The Spiral Of Words

Jorge Armenteros

Spuyten Duyvil
New York City

© 2019 Jorge Armenteros

ISBN 978-1-949966-38-1

Library of Congress Cataloging-in-Publication Data

Names: Armenteros, Jorge, author.
Title: The spiral of words / Jorge Armenteros.
Description: New York : Spuyten Duyvil, 2019. |
Identifiers: LCCN 2019025083 | ISBN 9781949966381 (paperback)
Subjects: LCSH: Authorship--Fiction. | LCGFT: Experimental fiction.
Classification: LCC PS3601.R5723 S65 2019 | DDC 813/.6--dc23
LC record available at https://lccn.loc.gov/2019025083

"Words are symbols for shared memories."

—Jorge Luis Borges

Part I
The Writer

He walked often. He walked because new words did not find him and the spent ones stuck to his skin. So he often walked. And the path became a river, and the waters burned. And every step was nothing but a dream. So he plunged… deeply.

Sometimes walking really meant propelling himself forward by the elliptical cadence of hips, knees, ankles, and toes. Other times it meant staying firmly grounded but letting his mind drift ahead rhythmically, one thought after the other, in a march towards the unknown, towards those oblique words that had yet to own him. That kind of walk was dangerous.

By this time the air had awoken, and the sun was assailing the beach. He had already reached the Pointe de Rauba-Capeù, and when he turned around to take in the view, he realized his thoughts had walked past him and were playing by themselves. He shook his head, sat down on the stone parapet, and listened to the waves crest over and throw themselves against the rocks. If the sea did not have to return to where it came from, neither did he. So he just sat there and watched as the wave of humans emerged from La Prom' and passed by him, some walking, some running, all dreaming, of course, all apparently going somewhere. Even the seagulls were fluttering up and down in a sort of a frenzy as if the air was burning them.

In front of him, the vast sea lay almost supple. Except for a few white crests frolicking in the horizon, the sea was essentially unmoved by his personal need for moving. And perhaps that was the reason for his need to see the sea, to see the sea eternal, always occupying the same space while violent currents flowed within its body. He looked up and focused on the line where the blue of the sea met the blue of the sky and wondered how long would it take him to get there. If he were to walk on water, would he ever reach that mythical juncture? Or would the line move away from him with every watery step? He looked hard and tried to sustain his gaze, but the intense solar reflection felt like a silver sword, blinding him. So he closed his eyes and followed the steps of his mind.

How is today different from any other day? Who cares if I finish my novel today? How many pages should I write? For how long should I walk? How many steps should I take? I can walk the beach from end to end, and then what? Yes, I can climb the chateau hill and leave the beach behind. But then I'll see the beach at the foot of the mountain, like a recumbent half moon, and I know I'll feel the need to walk on its edge. The edge pulls me, that edge formed by the white foam. Sometimes the edge of a sidewalk drags me along, sometimes the edge between light and darkness. Between the known and the unknown, there's an edge, and it also pulls me along… Look at the people coming and going down La Prom'. I wonder what motivates them. Maybe the desire to feel the open space. Maybe no desire at all, just a habit. Too many minds out there, who knows what they're thinking? Who cares, when I start walking, everything changes and I forget why I started.

After a few minutes of contemplation, he got to his feet and started retreating to the other end of the beach where the sun was on its way down, splashing red everywhere. He did not live on the west side of town, but finding himself far out there would force him to walk back to the old port where he rented a small flat behind a flaming red façade. And then the dusk grew immense. A million lights on the buildings lining La Prom' began to form yet another edge leading him along. And at that unexpected moment, a woman wearing a pair of tight running shorts and a loose shirt joined his rhythmic walk at an uncomfortably close distance. He did not know this woman. He kept walking at the same pace and pretended to ignore her. And they walked side-by-side for about a hundred meters until he stopped his march abruptly. She also stopped. They examined each other. He felt her uneasy eyes scanning him. Then he asked her what was she trying to do. And she answered that she was not trying to do anything. The little lights from the buildings cast a strange brilliance on her. He stepped back and tried to capture her full nature. But her nature was not evident; she had an elusive nature. She then started to walk away from him at a brisk pace, and he clearly noticed three red stars tattooed on her right ankle. He followed her down the boulevard for a while until she descended to the pebbles on the beach and ran into the incoming sea without taking off her clothes. At a healthy pace, she swam into the body of the sea until the waves swallowed her completely. And that was all he saw of her.

He sat on one of the blue chairs that lined the beach-front and continued to scan the sea. Nothing splashed, nothing moved. For a moment he feared the woman had drowned, but that preoccupation did not last too long. If she took to swimming, she must have known how to swim, he thought. He looked up to the sky and found it becoming, that is, he found it dark enough, yet luminous. Once again on his feet, he continued his journey back to the old port.

But his steps felt heavy as if he was dragging something. Did that woman drown? Was he carrying her dead body?

Once he reached the old port and sat in an Irish pub, he ordered the first pint of beer and set his eyes on the lazy boats. While absorbing the refracted and devilish light bouncing from the brightly painted hulls, his preoccupations began to melt away. He had completed his walk, traversed the terrain, and interacted with others from whom he managed to detach. Alone he was, or solitary, or simply free from human encumbrances. He was a single entity, a creature of the land of one, an essential element free to extend his travels unburdened. He was all to himself. And there lay the tragedy, the frailty—the strangeness.

The second pint of beer reminded him that in two days he was supposed to travel west. West and south to be precise, to the conflicted capital of Portugal and its haunting river. And he knew the trip was not mandatory, although it felt like a primordial need. He had promised himself to explore living and writing at the edge of Iberia with the great Atlantic Ocean at his back. He wanted to write prose on the verge, on the verge of meaning, on the verge of gravity, on the verge of nothingness. He wanted to write dangerously. The great explorers had left the shores of Iberia behind and leapt into the unknown. Likewise, he was looking to catapult his prose out into the tumultuous ocean, hoping to reach a new shore. And while considering what that prose would sound like, he managed to forget about the woman who went swimming.

And as he dreamt of his future discoveries, an intense chill cut through him when the body of a woman, the same woman he saw swimming into the sea, stood in front of him, blocking his view of the sailboats in the old port. He closed his eyes and pretended her presence did not bother him. But when he opened his eyes again, there she was, in her entirety, wearing the same attire, wet now, and somewhat wanting. He took a good swig from his pint and laid on her the thickest gaze possible. But the woman did not move; she just stood still and returned his gaze with the intensity of a jackal.

She asked him what his name was and he said, Calixto. But that was not his real name. That was his pen name. The real one, the one given to him at the baptismal fountain, he did not share with her. In reality, his real name was not known by anyone who knew him.

She sat next to him and ordered a pint. She also looked out to the sailboats, perhaps in an attempt to identify with his interests, when most likely she had no particular affinity for sailing. But when the waitress brought her a sweaty pint to the table, she raised it and toasted to the brave sailors and the muses that hide under the surface of the sea which she just came from visiting. And the fact that water was dripping all over the table from her long hair and wet clothes did not seem to bother her. She raised her pint again and proclaimed that her name was Lulu and that she knew about the sea and its inhabitants. She then said that nothing new ever emerged from the dry surface of the land, that the sea was the true incubator of life and creativity, that all things worthwhile originated from its depths, and that if he wanted to write anything worthwhile he needed to take to the sea. He listened to her attentively, and after those comments, he took another good swig from his pint. They remained silent, although they finished their respective pints right in front of each other.

I wonder if I know this woman. Not her physical self—I've never seen her before—but her soul. There's a familiar gravity to her gestures and her confident manner. Maybe I've written about her. She could have been a character. No, I don't think so, she never got into one of my novels. But how could she know I want to write something worthwhile? Perhaps she is known to one of my characters, in which case, I may know something about her. But my characters don't share everything with me. Sometimes they lie. That happens when I lose control, and they run ahead of me, ahead of the story. I really don't know what the characters do when they jump outside of the story. Nevertheless, I think I've come across this intrepid soul before.

On the horizon, numerous white sails crisscrossed the unending blue, signaling the near end of the afternoon regatta. He focused on the action far away, away from Lulu, away from his rumination. Everything that had to happen would happen far away. And today was clearly not different from any other day, so he tried to disconnect from the moment and think of the upcoming trip to Lisbon. He could touch the brume climbing up from the banks of the Tejo, flooding the Praça do Comércio and the old streets nearby, confusing the seagulls. And at once, mounting an attack he did not expect, reality interrupted his daydreaming. Lulu got up from her chair, left a few euros on the table, made her way down the quay of the old port, and kept on walking until she disappeared onto a side street. And that was all he saw of her and the three red stars tattooed on her ankle.

The next day, early in the morning, Calixto considered walking along the same route as in the previous day. Probably because he hoped to see Lulu again. But deep in his mind, he knew things usually did not repeat themselves. If he were to replicate the actions of the previous day, everything would turn out completely different. For that reason, he discarded the idea of walking along the beach. He wanted to allow for the possibility of running into Lulu—by chance. He did not trust chance at an intellectual level, but viscerally, he surrendered to it.

There was the chateau hill with a system of paths circling around it, bringing people from the street level all the way up to the top of the hill. There was also the confusing maze of streets in the old town. Together, those two sets of convoluted paths allowed him to walk in concentric circles for as long as he wanted without getting anywhere. But the problem with those routes was precisely that, the getting nowhere. Calixto rejected the absence of a destination on the principle that walking was more than just walking; there had to be some kind of displacement. If physical displacement did not happen, at least there had to be a displacement of the mind. So walking in circles around the chateau hill would clearly set his mind in motion, or in search of Lulu, or perhaps in search of the vagaries of chance.

Soon after breakfast, he emerged from the red façade looking firmly ahead. He set out at a comfortable pace, ignoring the faces of a multitude of people walking along, around, or against him. The air felt thin enough to encourage a faster pace, but he did not hurry. What needed to move fast were his thoughts, and they were indeed racing. Leaving the old port behind, he took the path at the bottom of the hill and started his ascent. After completing two full circles, just as the path became steeper, he saw the silhouette of a woman walking ahead of him and turning left at a bifurcation. He stopped walking at once. The resemblance between this unexpected silhouette and that of Lulu was remarkable, and he immediately knew he needed to make up his mind. Should he turn and follow the vanishing figure or should he keep on walking straight ahead?

Could it be her? Could it really be her? She looks very similar to Lulu, but from this point, I can't tell for sure. If I turn left at the bifurcation and walk faster, I'll catch up with this woman. I'll then find out if it's really her. But then, this won't be a chance encounter because I'm pursuing her. I'm supposed to find her by chance, not by design. But perhaps it was by chance that I saw her turn left at the bifurcation. If it's really her, the chance event already took place the moment she crossed my path before turning one way or the other. But there's no way for me to know for sure. So, what already happened clarifies nothing. If at the bifurcation I turn right instead of left and then find her at a later time, that would be a chance encounter. Or maybe everything is exactly the opposite of what I think it is, a perverse antithesis of my expectations. And of course, there's the rare possibility, that one dictated by chance, that I won't find her at all.

When he reached the forking he took a long look down the path veering left. He could see far enough to realize that although crowded with people, the path offered nothing for him. So he turned right and took his chances. At a faster pace he walked, hoping to gain on the possibility of an encounter. After a few meters, the gradual incline of the terrain brought him to a new height from where he could see the shore stretching west. There, he paused to admire the parallel edges of sea, sand, people, promenade, and buildings clinging to each other—all inseparable. Resisting the urge to linger there and dream of a distant shore, he continued climbing and hoping. He passed by hundreds of agave plants, rows of pine trees, beggars, lovers, children, and dogs without stopping or paying much attention to any of that, only fantasizing about that furtive silhouette. He pushed forward until reaching the top of the hill. There he stopped. He caught his breath. And not seeing Lulu or any other image that could resemble hers, he wept a little. Once again, he found himself alone. Chance evaded him, more precisely, his expectations of the miracles of chance were shattered. Even though he was at the highest point of the village, he felt as if he had descended into a deep hole. He lifted his head and looked forward. The coiling path that would take him back to where he started from awaited his descent. And there he stood, almost paralyzed, when the floodgates of his mind opened.

A while back, in a place where the hills were covered by moss, my steps fell silent. And silence is what I need, now when the voices of those who walked ahead are calling me. I hear the poets saying there's no path, that we make our path as we walk. I hear my characters, the brave ones who dare to exist outside my realm, calling me. I hear the inner voice hammering hard, propelling me to move on. But now I yearn for silence to mourn the loss of Lulu, a person I barely know. Or perhaps I mourn the loss of her image, that image that walks away from me. I also need to mourn the loss of chance. For all of these losses I need silence, but I see no moss to quiet everything down. So I'll circle down the hill to the edge of the old town. I'll walk through the maze of twisting streets, plazas, and churches. I'll retreat behind the red facade of my flat. I'll close the windows. And once silence finally rains on me, I'll try to forget that walkers bury their hopes under the dust of forsaken towns.

The rest of the day disappointed him deeply. With no more walking to do, he resigned to prepare for the trip to Lisbon the next morning. A new shore would provide a new vision of life, and perhaps, new prose. Words would be born in new ways, he hoped. But his enthusiasm was obliterated by the sense of loss he had experienced that morning. So he decided to try to forget everything that happened in the last two days by finishing packing and reading a few passages from Clarice Lispector's *Água Viva*. He floated in the words for a few minutes. The water was cold, and so was his memory of Lulu, or the image of Lulu.

*****

On the way to Lisbon, Calixto considered leaving behind anything that could potentially drag him down. He inspected his suitcase, carefully evaluating every item with a draconian eye. But the content of the suitcase was minimal, so he found no reason to castigate himself. His mind, however, contained a more complex inventory: many doubts, including profound insecurity and a significant amount of self-pity. Those thoughts slowed him down that fine morning. Had he not rushed out of his flat, he would have missed his flight to Lisbon. Aware of the time constraints, he called a taxi, grabbed on to his copy of Àgua *Viva*, and ventured into the conflicted unknown.

Lisbon was not new to him; he had already tasted its delicacies; he had already abused its offerings. But living in Lisbon as a writer was completely different. The Tejo made its presence felt season after season; it lived the life of a redolent corpse. And even if he wanted to ignore the Tejo's influence, the river infiltrated the very fiber of every living cell in Lisbon. And he was prepared for the abuse, for no extraneous forces ever made a dent on him. Or so he thought on that fine afternoon when he finally descended into the streets of Old Lisbon.

Without a clear destination, he ventured into the heart of the city singing a private song. He wanted to open his mind and heart to everything the old city had to offer. He wandered freely, unbound, taking in the weeping colors of the old façades, the acrid smell of people and buildings, and the tired afternoon miasma. But his enthusiasm was hindered by the water molecules and their maleficent agenda. Those moist molecules ascended directly from the superficial layers of the Tejo, high into the middle winds that caressed the myriad town hills, extending themselves supremely until they finally landed with aplomb on anything human, animal, mineral, or vegetal, injecting moisture into everything they touched. And as a consequence, a strange sweat grew from every surface. Even as he avoided touching anything, he could smell the moisture, and that disturbed him.

At the Praça do Rossio, he found a chair and a table from where he could write on his laptop and watch the human intercourse. People transacted, lied, exploited, exalted, exhausted, and loved each other. People behaved as people behave. And somehow he knew that this would help his writing, for the visceral exchange between people cannot be invented. As a writer of challenging prose, the raw interactions between human beings had to be recreated, not softened or diluted but rendered as true with whiskers and tails.

The human river poured down in front of him. People of various colors invaded the plaza at a frenetic pace, suggesting the world was coming to an end. But there was no end nearby; to the contrary, the world was blossoming. And in his mind, the words were brewing. He abandoned all preconceptions and launched himself into the creative process. Without a predetermined path or a preconceived plot, he ventured into the unknown, peering down into the abyss, and then tried to release the river of words.

Soon into the writing process, before the prose had a chance to twist and turn, he came across the image of Lulu. His fingers froze. He stopped writing at once. A woman had crossed the plaza from corner to corner bearing an uncanny resemblance to Lulu. He looked at the woman and wondered if that could be her, in Lisbon, walking right in front of him. He considered the absurdity of that thought. And after convincing himself that she was nowhere in that plaza, he tried to start writing again.

*****

Calixto wrote lies mainly, not because he wanted to deceive anyone, far from the truth, but because he thought that reality was as much a lie as any good fiction. He absorbed reality as it undressed in front of him. He took it all deep inside his mind and body. But somehow he found reality questionable, not entirely truth-worthy, even when it screamed and flapped its arms. He was suspicious of the way life needed to convince us of its force, of its existence. And with a certain disdain for anything real, he wrote prose that took flight, a flight as real as any presumptive reality.

Once he wrote the first sentence that afternoon, a sentence that had no reason to exist other than its sudden appearance on the blank computer screen, a sentence that read, *there is no path, you forge the path as you go,* that very moment he decided to stand up and merge with the flow of people traversing the plaza. First, he walked among the crowd with no clear direction. But as soon as he got a glimpse of the various medieval streets radiating away from the plaza, he turned left and walked onto one of them. He did not know where he was going, but the street felt so welcoming that he could not help but to smile and hop like a child. Not expecting anything, not succumbing to a prescribed order, his senses were free to register life anew. He heard words, music, and mopeds sounding like frenetic mosquitoes. He saw shadows, light reflected from store windows, colors copulating. He felt the dampness in the air. And then he was surprised by the aroma of freshly baked bread. He followed the olfactory invitation inside a bakery where people were queuing to purchase their daily loaf.

This must be the smell of life. I don't know how else to describe this sensation. So simple, yet so deeply rooted inside my brain. Bread can keep me alive, or maybe I'm alive so I can eat bread. So powerful, so elemental. And it doesn't matter where I am, what city, what continent. This smell burs inside of me and reaches the core of my existence. More compelling than bliss, more potent than fear. I think of bread as the primordial substance. The man makes bread so he can continue to be a man who eats bread. Circular, never-ending...

Inside the bakery, standing in line to grab a piece of life, the person immediately behind him, a woman unknown to him until that moment, asked him if he was a writer. He admitted he was a writer and ignored the uncanniness of the question. This he did because he was under the succulent influence of the aromas swirling inside the shop. He could not grasp the strangeness of the situation. But once outside, before he had the opportunity to taste a piece of the baguette he had just purchased, the woman approached him again and asked him what kind of writer he was. Looking at her, appreciating her angular features, noticing that she also held a baguette under her arm, he told her that he was a writer of lies. She did not flinch. She continued looking at him with an unfamiliar face. And after digging into the well of recent and remote memories, he concluded he had never seen or spoken to this woman before. But somehow she knew, or at least sensed, something about him that was true. And that capability to elucidate the unknown disarmed him. They both stood there on the sidewalk, each holding their respective baguettes, unsure of what to say or where to go next.

The impasse did not last long, for they both started walking down the street in the same direction, side-by-side, occupying the entire width of the sidewalk. People who came up the sidewalk needed to step into the street to pass by them, while those coming from behind found their path blocked. And this continued for a few blocks until they reached the formidable banks of the Tejo where they were swallowed by its miasmatic breath. Still intrigued, Calixto cut the curtain of fog with his words. He told her that he wrote about lies not because he feared the truth, but because he did not really know what the truth was. She listened to him attentively and then she broke off the tip of the baguette and proceeded to savor the crunch of life. After thinking about his declaration and chewing on the bread, she told him that the bread was excellent and that she had no interest in the veracity of things either. She then asked him what led him to be a writer. And this he did not answer. Instead, he considered asking how did she know he was a writer in the first place. But concerned about the potential answer she would give him, he decided to abort that question completely. Alternatively, he asked if she would join him for a cup of coffee. She said that she would love to join him as long as he would not ask her if she was a writer herself. He agreed, and he wondered.

They soon found a café with a terrace on the sidewalk overlooking people and cats. Calixto sat far enough from her not to appear threatening but close enough to feel her intriguing presence. She asked for a coffee, but he did not follow his own suggestion and asked for a glass of Alentejo. Once she took the cup of coffee and brought it to her lips, he clearly saw three words tattooed on the inner side of her right forearm. They were written in a beautiful typeface with elegant twirling serifs. But he could not recognize the language nor could he decipher the meaning of the words. And when she took another sip from her cup, the words danced in front of him, begging for interpretation. Considering that she did not want to be asked if she was a writer, he concluded that asking what the words meant would be equally forbidden. So he did not ask anything at all. She clearly noticed that he was looking directly at her tattoo, and as if instigating his curiosity, did not bother to cover it.

After taking another piece of the baguette, dipping it in her coffee with delicacy, and savoring it thoroughly, she asked him what was the true nature of a lie. He was not prepared for that question. He fumbled. A lie was a lie. A lie was something with no foundation in the truth. A lie was a pretense. But then he said a lie was anything we say at any moment in any place. This sent him on a line of thought he wanted to avoid. But he continued and told her lying was not different from telling the truth. She reflected on this answer and asked him if he was lying to her that very moment. He said he was, indeed. Again she did not flinch.

She says nothing. I tell her that my words are false and she says nothing. Maybe her words are false as well. How can I tell? I really don't lie, I just write the things that come to my mind, often unadulterated, but ultimately honest. Honest in the sense that I don't fabricate on purpose. Yes, what I write isn't necessarily bound to anything tangible. But isn't that the nature of fiction? She was the one asking if I was a writer. Can she smell the lies? Possibly not, because I was the one volunteering that what I write are lies. She didn't say that, I did. But why would she preclude me from asking her if she is herself a writer? Could it be that she doesn't want to lie to me? Maybe one liar is more than enough. There's danger in repetition whether we're telling the truth or not. She may sense that. And then her arm is branded with words I cannot decipher. I could ask her what those words mean. But what if she plainly lies to me? Would it make a difference? The truth is that she knows something about me and I only know that I know nothing about her. Only that she likes bread, that seems to be true.

The next gesture took him by surprise. Without asking for approval, permission, or anything, she reached for his baguette and took a piece of it, dipped it in her coffee, and swallowed it at once. She was pensive for a few seconds and then told him that his baguette was just as tasty as hers. In her face he found no trace of concern, not a line of preoccupation, it was placid, still, like the waters of a lake in the morning. Tempted as he was to respond, he could not find what to say to her, so he had some of his wine, stood up momentarily, and then sat down again and acted as if nothing had happened. Calixto knew that something was happening, but he could not put his finger on what it was.

She then called the waitress and asked for a glass of Alentejo as well. Once served, she raised the glass and toasted to the vagaries of life. When Calixto asked her what vagaries she was referring to, she said that none were coming her way lately and that she was hoping for that to change. She went on to explain that their encounter at the bakery was not unpredictable enough, that she had expected it would happen like that. Not convinced, he questioned her if in reality she already knew about their encounter or was she just trying to explain her peculiar behavior. She took a while to respond, the faintest of lines crossed her forehead, and she slightly tilted her head as if perplexed almost. With a tone, impassive and inscrutable, she said her behaviors were not peculiar, that to him perhaps they were, but not so to the universe. This exchange led to a silence that hung from a low cloud.

The afternoon continued its relentless advance. Fearing that the hours would engulf him in the company of this puzzling woman, and also fearing that she would not reveal much, he felt compelled to press for answers. He jumped into the abyss of the unknown and asked about the meaning of the words tattooed on her forearm. He knew he was taking a risk, but could not appreciate its magnitude. After listening to his question, she looked at the words and contemplated them with tenderness, as if they revealed a sweet memory. She then pronounced each word in a soft voice, almost caressing each syllable. When she finished speaking she stared at him, and he saw, once again, the still waters of a morning lake. But still, he did not understand what the words meant. The language sounded completely foreign to him, a beautiful sound he had never heard before. And when he asked her what did the words really mean, she said that the meaning rested in the words themselves and that she had just spoken them to him.

First Lulu, then this woman whose name I don't even know. These encounters taking place in two different cities, back to back, within days of each other. Is this chance? She may simply disappear, vanish into the brume. Or she could sit across from me, as she does now, and speak in a language I don't under-

stand. The words have their intrinsic music but no meaning to me. Perhaps her appearance demonstrates there's no inherent meaning to those words, that the sound and emotion they elicit is all there's to have. I'm not ready to accept that notion, not when my life still revolves around words. What's truly disturbing is the fact that she seems to know something about me when I have no idea about who she is.

Then the lightning, a white so fast but so decisive, turning the afternoon into a theater with a torn curtain, a deep rip down to the edge of the waters, and a river that flowed quick and away. They both marveled at the spectacle. The sound followed, call it thunder, but to them, it was more a like a roar. The words had no chance against the roar. He knew not to challenge the might. She, instead, kept on talking. Her words did not reach his ears, drowned they were by the thunderous roar. But the silent elliptical movement of her lips caught his eyes. Calixto could not decipher what she was saying. But the movement, the act of uttering, the giving birth to that unknown language, made him grab the seat of his chair and contain himself from embracing her, or from running away from her. The lightning continued, completely unaware of what both of them were thinking or wanting.

Then the rain, enormous, as if the river had fallen from the sky. They got up from the table, grabbed their respective half-eaten baguettes, and moved inside the café seeking shelter. But what shelter could they find when the wheels of the mind had already started to turn? The cramped space inside the café forced them to breach the tenuous line of the impersonal. Convinced that she knew a world about him, Calixto was surprised when she asked his name. This time her words were clear and direct. But when he tried to answer, he fumbled the words and failed to say his name. A faint smile grew on her face, a peaceful smile. She then turned away from him and began to contemplate the falling rain. He feared she would simply vanish and be one with the water. But he also feared she would not vanish at all, in which case, he would have to reveal to this person more about himself when she was not revealing anything about herself. He lied, while she was still looking out at the rain, when she could not scrutinize his face, he told her his name was "Calixto." She remained quiet for a moment, a moment that dragged for a century, before speaking to the rain and saying that "Calixto" was not his real name.

Calixto did not mind shifting paradigms. He accepted darkness at noon. He even welcomed the world upside down. But, most often, he was the author of the chaos in his life. The sweet taste of the unknown suited him well, as long as there was a safety net underneath it all. So what he could not bear that moment was the certainty of the uncertain woman. She seemed unperturbed and placid, inquisitive and yet accepting. And somehow, somehow she knew something about him. He then remembered the first sentence he had written earlier at the plaza: *there is no path, you forge the path as you go.* So he stood up from the chair and started walking away from this woman he could not unriddle, his baguette getting completely soaked under his arm under the relentless rain.

After walking aimlessly for several hours, Calixto finally reached the hotel room he had secured upon his arrival in Lisbon. It was 10 pm. That was a good time to continue writing and expanding on that first sentence he wrote at Praça do Rossio. The night was young, but young only in the sense of time, for nights have existed forever so nothing about a night could really be nubile. However, the immediacy of his need was truly nubile. And his need walked along two parallel paths: a strong desire to create meaningful prose on one side; and just next to this noble need, a nagging urge to find out about this woman who shared with him a baguette and the rain. Anyone could have been conflicted when deciding which path to choose, but he knew not to take sides, he simply thought hard about the fleeting images of the woman while he typed a few loose sentences in his computer. He managed to do just that for a few minutes, he then walked over to the small kitchenette in the hotel room and poured himself a glass of Alentejo. Back at the computer, he read the sentence he had just written. Ashamed of the baseness of the language and the poverty of the images, he closed his computer and walked over to the window to look outside. The view was magnificent, open and dark, even vulnerable. And he looked into the night like a hunter. But the night basically ignored him. Like any other night, this one continued to deepen its shades of gray, to relax its grip on common anxiety, and to gather the first droplets of hue.

Two women had brutally intersected his life while he was simply being, or walking, or just having a piece of bread. All within the last few days. He considered the inherent anomaly of these two encounters, and before accepting them as fate, or even luck, he resolved to integrate the bizarre events into his writing. Not an easy task since all he had accomplished during the day was to write a single sentence. He considered how to best represent the oddity of both encounters. Lulu cast a spell, an image, a presence that still surrounded him. The woman at the bakery had no name, but somehow, she knew what his name was not and that he was a writer. And without saying much, that woman sent him into the rain and left him wondering what had just happened. That was powerful, he thought. And after searching for the right words and the right sentence structure, after writing and re-writing a few sentences in his mind, he felt defeated. So he abandoned the idea of writing anything at all.

He took to the night, the night that had no regard for him. He opened it like a moon ray would open any night. He pierced its layers. He walked into the vast space between the dark pavement and the dark sky. And as he walked into that emptiness, his steps felt equivocal, the ground moved, his legs failed to support his body erect. So he fell down, on his knees first, on his side next, and finally on the ground. There he lay, over the dark pavement under the dark sky, wondering what had brought him down; but more precisely, or even more intimately, how to write anything from this position?

Having had those thoughts before, he knew to ignore them. He eventually managed to stand up, like the capable man he was, and to start walking towards the river. If the night would yield to his needs, it would likely do so by the river. Once he regarded the expansive body of the Tejo, he realized it shared the same dark shades as the pavement and the sky. Relief was nowhere to be found there. And this is when he, once again, engaged in walking. He walked. He followed a circular path that spiraled away from the river, larger and larger with each turn. He kept a steady pace and tried to forget all that took place during the day. He walked ahead, always bearing left and keeping his head high. And this is all he did until the early morning came to greet him. He did not applaud when the sun showed its face. He felt tired, and not more enlightened than the day before. Walking the entire night had not provided any rewards. He did not get any revelations. He was simply spent.

But once he looked around and recognized the neighborhood, once he identified the color on the façades, and once he was assaulted by the aroma of freshly baked bread, an assault he recognized and cherished, he knew where to direct his steps. He followed his olfactory senses until he came to the same bakery he had visited the day before. There he stood in line hoping for a piece of heaven, but also hoping for a fresh acquaintance with the woman who knew what his name was not. When his turn came up, he said to the attendant that he was not ready to order and asked her to take care of the person behind him in the line. He used this newly acquired time to look around wishing to find the mysterious woman again. But nobody in the line, or around the bakery resembled the woman from the previous day. This he found disconcerting, for he expected the inquisitive woman to visit the bakery every single day.

Although his expectations had come into question, he remained in line and accepted his turn once it presented again. He asked for a baguette. The attendant acknowledged his request and said that it was good to see him again, that they did not often get writers as customers. He smiled, took his baguette, and quickly left the store. Once on the street, he stood still with his baguette under his arm. That was when he started breathing hard and fast. How could this woman, a young employee at a bakery, know that he was a writer? How was it possible that random people in Lisbon had knowledge of his profession? Clearly, the mysterious woman from the previous day must have spoken to the attendant, conveying his personal information. But he could not be certain that those two people had spoken to each other or shared any information about his writing. Why would that be relevant?

He stepped aside from the sidewalk to allow the flow of pedestrians to proceed with their morning routine. But as he stood in front of the adjacent storefront, he could not help but gaze at his own image reflected in the window. There he was, in all his reality, the very image of himself. He took a long time scrutinizing every angle in his face; he tried different facial expressions, some grotesque, others more affable. He moved forward and backward to study different details of his body. When two women came close to him on the sidewalk, he stopped all strange contorting in order to appear normal. But once they walked away, he continued with his private performance. After a while, he concluded that his appearance could not actually reveal that he was a writer. So, if the attendant at the bakery had that impression, it had to have been communicated by the strange woman he met the previous day, whose name he did not know, but to whom he admitted that he was, indeed, a writer.

Tired as he was, missing sleep, missing a sense of certainty, he decided to return to his hotel room in search of rest and restoration. Restoration of a sense of order for what he had considered to be obviously clear, like the lack of revealing details in his appearance, had all of a sudden come into question. Once he found himself in the safety of his hotel room, he considered writing the next few sentences of his book. But what he feared most, what he hoped never to face again, resurfaced all at once. He found himself watching himself as a writer while writing. This, an image he did not appreciate, so intimate, so uncomfortable.

So he worked fast to concoct a few sentences he doubted would ever make it into his next book. Not because the sentences were flawed, but because they were constructed under pressure. Instead of writing for the sense of discovery, he was writing out of fear. Not writing would certainly usher a heavy emptiness, or perhaps destroy the images of the two women he had now carried in his head for the last few days. In either case, the sense of writing under pressure overwhelmed the simple sense of pleasure, so he stopped at once. He took a piece of the baguette and savored the beauty of its construction. He then had another piece.

*****

In the early morning, Calixto was completely immersed in the sound of silence. A sound composed of nothing except minimal sprinkles of bird songs. The birds cared not for the silence but for their sex appeal and procreation success. So they sang energetically in the late morning. They were sparrows after all.

As soon as a deviant ray of sunlight penetrated through the window, biting a chunk of his leg, he opened his eyes and realized the day was upon him. And this day made its presence known immediately, for it brought forward all the possible words a language could contain, and at the same time, it presented all the limitations a mind could encounter when forging such a language. He felt the pressure. With conviction, he sat on his bed and held his body still for a few minutes. And only when he believed the world would open up to him, only when he sensed the words would be at his reach, he then got out of bed to listen to the singing sparrows.

After listening to a few melodic phrases, the urge to walk began to infiltrate his consciousness, leaving very little room for any other concern. He resisted the urge. He wanted to enjoy the simple pleasure of writing freely, writing unencumbered in the morning hours, writing with a background of bird songs. But in a matter of minute, he found himself walking down the street in front of his hotel with no clear idea as to were to go. He could still hear the birds that comforted him, but he knew that writing had died for the morning, or maybe for the entire day. Freedom and surprise would need to emerge from the act of walking. So he embraced that thought and continued his march. One crossroad followed another; some stores were bursting with people while others were desolate, people and dogs, but nothing that would ignite his curiosity. That was when he made a right turn onto a narrow street that climbed at a puzzling steep angle. The allure of following the tight corridor to a sort of heaven above drove him forward. He climbed fast, skipping steps. And after about a hundred meters, he reached a clearing that opened up in front of him, a truly profound openness.

*****

The midday sun fell hard on his hat. Calixto stood as straight as he could to prevent the burning rays from touching his body. The slightest movement or leaning would have exposed him. But standing was not walking, and that presented the biggest challenge. He considered waiting around for an hour or two before taking the next step. The sun would have moved a few degrees west allowing him to angle his hat and walk under the precarious shade. He decided to wait. To amuse himself as he waited, he tried to remember word by word the last paragraph he wrote before leaving Nice. He could not remember the words. He remembered the concepts and the tone of the sentences, but not the words. If the words did not remain in his memory, did they matter? He recognized the nefarious self-doubt at once. So, enduring the burning rays that attacked his body in motion, he set out to continue his walk, away from self-doubting thoughts, and toward the edge of the Tejo.

The river surprised him. He looked at it expecting a deep gray frown. But the river did precisely the opposite; it smiled at him. He waited for the river to flow, to take its course, to serpent at a continuous speed out to the ocean. And the river did just that. But when he regarded the visible expression of the river, when he saw the wind-induced ripples, the undulating wake of sailboats, the surface wounds inflicted by white birds, he was again surprised to find a lingering smile. Accepting the message, if there was any message in that vision, he turned away from the river. And without doubt in his mind, he started looking at people's faces expecting to find a legion of smiles. He found a few, not necessarily directed at him, but encouraging enough. That ignited his forward march once again. Across the Praça do Comércio he walked, this time displaying a smile of his own, inevitably eliciting further smiles from those he came across.

At a comfortable rhythm he traversed streets, he crossed a few plazas. A diagonal smile hung from his lips while he forged ahead following nothing but his instincts, or perhaps his olfactory sense fetched the smell of old leather and dust. And thereupon he arrived at the door of an old bookstore with a sign that read "Livraria Mundo." He stepped inside, careful not to alter the generations of dust covering the books on the display window. A young woman, sporting a colorful tattoo of a salamander on her neck, sat behind the sales counter reading a book. She looked up when he entered the store; the salamander did not move at all. Looking around he identified books from authors he recognized, and there were others he had never heard about, but they were lying around in no particular order. Walking through the empty store felt as if violating a private sanctuary, so after a few minutes he stopped meandering and asked the tattooed attendant if she could recommend a book for him. She first ignored him, but when he repeated his request in sketchy Portuguese, she looked at him and smiled but did not give an answer.

Erratic behaviors did not dissuade him from interacting with people, often random people, for he considered anything unusual the stuff of novels. So after browsing around for a little while longer, he returned to the sales desk and asked the attendant if she had a book about bread. This time the woman looked at him, caressed the salamander on her neck with the tip of her fingers, and once again said nothing. Bewildered, he remained standing in front of her and retained her gaze for a few seconds. The attendant bit her lower lip softly, caressed the salamander one more time, and turned her gaze down to the book she was reading. A deep silence took hold. Calixto then asked her what she was reading, but this time she did not even look up at him nor did she respond. He then turned around and headed for the exit. But just before stepping out on the street, he paused, he reconsidered the purpose of his walk, and convinced about the hidden liaisons operating in the universe, he returned to the sales desk. The young woman closed her book and stood up, the salamander calmly resting vertically between her chin and her collar bone. He asked again if she had a book about bread. The young woman nodded affirmatively and left the sales desk to enter into what seemed like a back-store office. She returned with a basket containing a couple of bread rolls which she placed on the sales desk right in front of him.

Calixto picked up one of the rolls and ate a piece of it. Instantly, he remembered the nameless woman he had met at the bakery, who knew he was a writer, and wondered if the tattooed woman who now offered him bread knew as much about him. After eating about half of the roll, he told the attendant that the bread was excellent but that he had asked for a book about bread, not for bread itself. She finally spoke with an accent that sounded Eastern European and said that real bread was better than a book about bread.

Not wanting to enter into a discussion about the signified versus the signifier, he finished eating the roll and almost agreed with her by saying that bread was the essence of life, but that life without books had no essence. She pondered his words, had a little piece of bread herself, and told him that he must be a writer, probably a novelist. He felt disarmed, revealed. He did not have a tattoo on his forehead that read "writer." He had not mentioned any specific authors. Maybe the titles of the books he perused gave him away. It could not have been the bread. Or was it?

Not wanting to confirm or deny her assertion, he attempted to turn the situation around by telling her that salamanders used to roam around freely all over the Carpathian Mountains before they were decimated by wars and bad weather. He guessed she would be a native of one of the many countries straddled by the fabled mountain range. When the attendant heard him mention the Carpathians, she touched the tattoo on her neck with the tips of her fingers, and the salamander appeared to twitch slightly. For an instant, he thought the salamander had stuck its tongue out to lick her fingers. But he soon dismissed the image and focused on her soft smile instead of the reptile. She appeared to be daydreaming or remembering something sweet. She then said in her peculiar accent that reptiles were found only in the lower altitudes and foothills of the Carpathians, that she came from the small village of Rakhiv, high up in Ukraine, where wolves were more common than salamanders. Then she added that he should visit Rakhiv, where he would find a lot to write about in his novels. This meant she did not speculate when suggesting he was a writer, she was certain he was one, and that thought disturbed him.

Calixto could not help but consider the inherent importance of the number 3. He found it mysterious, metaphysical, and magical. From time to time in the history of the world various numbers, chiefly those from 1 to 12, have been regarded as possessing mythical significance, but there can be no doubt that in the extent, variety, and frequency of its use the number 3 far surpasses all the rest. Aristotle's *Rhetoric* consisted of 3 books; the original Hydra had three heads, the *Dies Irae* is composed of 3x3x3 stanzas, each consisting of 3 verses and a triple rhyme, there were Three Graces, goddesses of such things as charm, beauty, and creativity, the scepter of Neptune was a trident. But more relevant to his immediate reality, three different women have inadvertently crossed his path and rattled his sense of self, purpose, and direction.

Unsure as to the meaning of anything at this point, he confessed to the attendant that he was indeed a writer and asked her if her name was Lulu. She smiled again, shook her head, and said nothing. Then she stepped around the sales counter and walked toward the shelf that contained newly released fiction from all over the world. With a gentle gesture, she pointed at various books without signaling one in particular. Then she asked him to identify his own novels. The chances that any of his books could be found in that bookstore were practically nonexistent, so he did not even try to look for them. When she saw he did not try, she asked him if he was afraid to actually find one of his books in the store. He was not afraid, and he told her so. With the same irresistible smile, she said her name was Lyubochka and that he should consider writing a book about her name. He hesitated, not entirely certain he wanted to unravel the mysterious and captivating presence she exuded, but driven to know more, he asked her for the meaning of her name. She said, *love… Perhaps love.*

At this point, Calixto knew his reality was under siege. Remaining at the store would have created situations capable of derailing his resolve to write. He realized Lyubochka had ignited his interest, that she had the capacity to distract him today and many more days to come. But he also understood that she was not different from the other two women that had recently captured his attention. They had materialized from nowhere, they had interacted with him, and they had departed leaving him baffled. Lyubochka, however, was still in front of him and had not vanished as the others had done. And maybe that made her irresistibly dangerous.

Calixto said that *love* was meaningful, that more people in the world should understand *love*, or experience it fully, or maybe make it the center of their lives. And he said all of this while walking towards the door, away from her, somewhat afraid he would believe exactly what he was saying. But before he managed to step out on the street, Lyubochka grabbed the remaining piece of bread and offered it to him. He could not resist. Life was bread and bread was life. So he tasted the product of the earth and sat at the steps of the store, half of his body leaning forward into the street, away from Lyubochka, and the other half wanting to stay behind to learn more about her.

But the urge to walk reverberating from within mounted a phenomenal attack on his immediate reality and dislodged him from the steps where his mind was indulging on everything Lyubochka. And he accepted the power of that inner drive, the destabilizing force it represented, the might it possessed. So he stood up, looked one more time at the salamander guarding Lyubochka's neck, and started to make his way down the street. She asked him if he was leaving for the day or leaving forever. He stopped, the road continued at a steep angle down toward the river that had delivered him with a smile earlier that day. He wanted to say he would come back at another time, that he needed to see her again. But he did not manage to promise anything; he only said that *love* had a meaning, a meaning that he could not yet understand.

*****

On his way back to the hotel, Calixto avoided bookstores and bakeries. On one occasion, after changing his course by two blocks just to bypass what seemed to be a bakery from a distance, he landed on a side street right in front of a small bookstore with foreign titles on display. He felt the temptation to go into the store and start browsing. But out of fear of the potential scenarios that could be unleashed, he turned around and headed in a new direction, away from the bookstore — changing his path while walking was not unusual for him. After all, his walks were predictably unpredictable. But making a change out of fear did not settle well with him. Any force, external or internal, could dictate the direction of his walks, except for the force of fear. Fear foretold disagreeable events that had yet to happen. Why endure the emotional turmoil of something that has not impacted our lives thus far? With that thought in mind, he changed his path once more, he backtracked and walked right into the small bookstore. Life would not be worth anything without facing fear and surprise, he thought.

This time he did not ask for any books, he did not look for bread, and he did not expect to meet any mysterious attendant. But reality was ready to usher the unexpected. And it did. On top of a reading table, in a pile of commercial novels, he identified one of his own books translated into Spanish. He was very proud of the Spanish translation but did not appreciate seeing his novel mixed with inane books ready for easy consumption. He felt wounded. Not finding a salesperson around, he rung the little bell on the sales desk several times. After a few minutes, an old man came up through a spiral staircase that possibly led to a cellar, and asked him if he was in need of help. Calixto was not in need of any help; he just needed to express his indignation. An indignation that had no bearing on the man that just emerged from the cellar, but perhaps on the natural order of things: finding his book piled among a divergent crowd. The old man, looking above the rim of his glasses, asked him if he had found what he came looking for.

To this question, Calixto could only answer that he did not really know what he was looking for, that he felt the drive to come into the store because the alternative was to yield to esoteric fears. Here the old man nodded, he seemed to understand his level of distress. Taking small steps, the old man moved towards Calixto and placed himself in front of the reading table displaying science fiction, romance, and detective novels. Feeling an uncomfortable pressure from the old man, Calixto took turns between looking at the books and looking sideways and upward at that carved face the old man presented. He then picked up the Spanish translation of his book entitled "*No Somos Pero Somos.*" He showed it to the old man and asked him if he had read it. Very quickly the old man responded that he had not read the book, that he could not read it as other people could. Not understanding what the old man meant, Calixto felt compelled to clarify that he was the author of the book. The old man took this information very seriously. He grabbed the book and paused to read the title again. He then started to turn one page after the other as if trying to find an important phrase or word. The old man closed the book and held it tight against his chest. He then looked straight into Calixto's eyes and said that he was very sorry for him, that if he could, he would take him as his son.

At that moment the afternoon light had changed in quality; it reflected the harshness of expectations while the building walls across the street emitted a hue akin to tired human flesh. This did not pass unaccounted, for the old man said the afternoon was testing. And it was, indeed. Calixto took the book from the old man's hands and told him that nothing was, but that everything was. He told him that he could be a son to no father, that he was happy to see his book on the table yet not seeing the book would have also been glorious. The old man listened attentively, his eyes on the book, probably not believing what he was hearing. And at this point, the old man grabbed the book again, tossed it away from sight, and pulled two chairs from the reading table. He placed one chair in front of the other. He then sat on one of them and invited Calixto to sit on the other one. He did.

The old man started talking about the brutal times of

Salazar when good books could not be sold openly when everything was censored. That was when he started selling books in translation because their "subversive" nature was not easily identified by the thugs who came around to inspect his inventory. Books in Spanish were still a risk, and so were those in French. But he could get away with almost anything written in German or English. The problem was not only obtaining such books but that once he had them, most of his clients in the resistance did not understand those languages. So he felt suffocated, the regime cutting off the source of illuminated words and critical thinking. He said that he started selling books that looked like real bibles. The cover and the first few pages in Portuguese, but experimental fiction in the core of the volumes. That was thanks to the artistry of an atheist bookbinder in Lisbon who delighted himself more by ripping the bible pages apart than by inserting the new experimental work. It was the sweet sense of desecration that emboldened him. He also spoke about the recent recession when nobody had any money for anything, let alone for buying books. He had to survive by selling newspapers that were reporting on the catastrophic financial situation of the country, which resulted in people feeling more anxious, which lead them to spend less every day and hurting his business more. So he stopped selling newspapers. And then he started talking about the importance of fiction in people's lives, how he enjoyed selling aesthetically adventurous literature. He spoke about how happy he was not to have to mask good literature as bibles anymore, that he could openly promote challenging, innovative works of high quality and exceptional ambition, how he hoped that the books he sold could, perhaps, alter people's perception of the world. He then quoted Clarice Lispector saying, *In order to write I must place myself in the void. In this void where I exist intuitively. But it's a terribly dangerous void: its where I wring out blood.* And then he asked Calixto if he ever felt that way.

After giving thoughtful consideration to everything the old man had said, and after reflecting on what he had done since arriving in Lisbon, Calixto admitted that, yes indeed, he was in a dangerous void. A void created by his need to walk, always leaving behind the known spaces to venture into the unknown. And in this frenetic need to move forward, he often wondered if valuable thoughts, experiences, or opportunities were continuously left behind, aborted, or simply ignored. That was not a comfortable thought for it implied careless waste and inefficiency. But a sense of void, as explained by Clarice Lispector, was not to be disregarded, to the contrary, the old man was squarely on the mark when he presented him with such a challenge. So admitting he was in the depths of a void felt like a relief, but not for too long, because the old man gave him no rest and immediately asked how was he going to remedy his situation. Calixto had not resolved what the next steps would be. He really did not know how to fill any void. In lieu of an answer, he spoke about an upcoming trip to a place he was not sure existed, but that if it did, his void would not be that empty after all. A critical smirk hung from the old man's lips when he heard this statement. He then took another good look at Calixto and said he was, undoubtedly, a writer.

Once again, the confrontation with his profession assaulted him. Not that Calixto aspired for anonymity, he actually revealed to the old man he was a writer, not that he wanted to hide from the judgmental eyes of readers or critics, nor was he avoiding the social responsibilities of a contemporary writer, nor was he attempting to deceive his interlocutors; but to be regarded as a genuine writer at once, based on minimal interaction, made him feel exposed. And he did what he could to maintain a neutral expression when facing the old man. He took a deep breath and gazed deeply into the old man's eyes, hoping to reveal what he really was: a conflicted writer and a walker in a dangerous void.

Without moving from his chair, the old man stretched his hand and grabbed a book from a low shelf next to him. He blew away the white dust that had accumulated on top of the book. He opened the book and read the following passage: *In order to write a single line, one must see a great many cities, people and things, have an understanding of animals, sense how it is to be a bird in flight, and know the manner in which the little flowers open every morning. In one's mind, there must be regions unknown, meetings unexpected and long-anticipated partings, to which one can cast back one's thoughts…* The old man closed the book. And with the most untroubled expression, he stared at Calixto for what seemed like a lunar year. The void deepened, and from its depths, Calixto managed to ask who was that writer who seemed to know his soul. The old man handed him the book. It was a very worn copy of Rilke's *The Notebooks of Malte Laurids Brigge*, a book Calixto had read many years ago with delight and had felt transmuted by its existential disquiet.

This man, this bookworm, seems to know me. How else could he have selected that passage? I must be transparent; he just read through me. Or maybe he has read some of my books and knows what haunts me. He sells books, he knows all writers confront turbulence. Every writer faces it in his or her own particular way, but turbulence nonetheless. Could the experience of writing be universal? Perhaps… But not the experience of walking. Everyone walks, but not everyone needs to walk. And certainly, not everyone needs to write and walk. That cannot be a universal necessity. I'm drawn to writing while I have an urge to walk. These two are different forces, and they impact me in different ways. I doubt other people feel it this way. However, this old man intuits that there is something, a force, a need, something, compelling me to do just that. But the more I think about him, the more I suspect he's also a writer. Or maybe we're all writers, all of us, the entire human species. We survive on words, don't we?

Calixto could not tolerate sitting in front of the old man much longer. Although he wanted to learn more about this person, about his ideas, about his experiences with other writers, and about his intuitive capacity, the urge to walk away impaled him. He stood up and headed towards the door. But before leaving behind the old man, Calixto told him that he wanted to come back at another time to sit in front of him again. The old man agreed, waved him goodbye, and told him to be careful with the sirens.

Gliding over century-old paving stones, Calixto made his way back to Praça do Rossio where he hoped to tap into the writing vein once more. He found the same café where he had written that one sentence. This time, however, he was determined to go deeper. Without a pen, notebook, or laptop; empty-handed as he was, Calixto went for the open sea. He swam into the turbulent waters of thoughts and recent events in search of the next phrase. Almost immediately he came across the images of Lulu, then the unnamed woman with whom he shared a baguette, then Lyubochka, and finally the old man in the bookstore. These were a great many people as suggested by Rilke, and he had certainly seen a great many cities. But in spite of having seen plenty, he was at a loss for that next single line. A sense of discomfort and uneasiness pounced on him. Calixto ordered a glass of ruby port hoping to soothe the pain. When the waiter brought him the dark-colored balsam, he did not allow him to place the glass on the table. Instead, he took it from the waiter's hands and drank half of it at once. He was not attempting to drown his consciousness; he only wanted to feel a little less. Emboldened, he swam deeper into his thoughts.

Calixto reminded himself that coming to Lisbon was an attempt to write prose on the verge, that he wanted to write dangerously. So he understood there was no need to fear fortuitous encounters with strangers. To the contrary, those were the pearls of his journey. Those accidents were the raw material for equally accidental prose. He had met those iconoclasts while randomly walking through the streets. This realization soothed him as much as the ruby port. And as the sense of discomfort loosened its grip, Calixto allowed himself to observe the unknown walkers that came to the Praça do Rossio. Some entered the plaza from around a corner, crossed it diagonally, and disappeared in haste. Others entered the space and felt compelled to turn in circles around the fountains. There were those who seemed to walk erratically. Yet there were those who came and stayed in the plaza for a while, only leaving after an internal force pushed them out.

But to some extent, the immense mass of walkers must have been affected by the black and white pattern of the floor in the plaza. That was the grid that bound their feet. And Calixto firmly believed that all of those walkers could tell a story about their walk in the plaza. Walking was movement, movement was life, and inevitably, life led to fiction.

The sun started to soften, the air started to divagate, and Calixto's thought process found a quiet moment. He regarded the river of people traversing the plaza and felt satisfied. A multitude of minds had no other purpose but to imagine. And imagination had the power to render the world anew, to uncover the unseen. And in the process of uncovering, risks would be taken; maybe language would be forged. And the forging of new language meant we had a future, in the words, in the inventiveness of the minds that write, and think.

*****

The morning did not wait for Calixto. By the time he managed to get dressed and step out the door, bread had been consumed all over Lisbon and sentences had been written by innumerable writers. He was unsure how that happened, but it had. And he knew because the air was impregnated with the smell of fresh baguettes and the sound of fresh words. Both were essential elements for him, for his life, so in that particular morning, he felt completely alive. He then started walking with the idea of creating a large spiral with his trajectory. To accomplish this, he only turned to the right while covering increasing distances before making a new turn. He wanted to avoid the constancy of a circle's diameter and the repetition that such constancy entailed. He wanted to experience a rotational force, ever growing, bringing him forward, but at the same time remaining linked to the essential elements at its center. He did not want to lose the sound of the words or the smell of fresh bread; he wanted to stretch their limits.

Calixto accepted the possibility of a chance encounter with any of the people he had met since arriving in Lisbon. That thought made him smile. So as he started to walk and turn, and to turn and walk, he scrutinized the faces of people he came across on streets and sidewalks, expecting a familiar face. There were many profiles that could have been confused with those of Lulu or Lyubochka, but none turned out to be the real Lulu or Lyubochka. About a block ahead, a man carrying a book under his arm waved at him. Calixto accelerated his pace to catch up with that man, but by the time he reached the corner, the man had already disappeared behind a massive wooden door. He wondered if that man could have been the owner of the bookstore. But all he saw was a gesture and none of his face so that man could have been anybody waving goodbye to anybody else on the street.

The streets in Lisbon had the mischievous habit of ascending and descending at will. Often, Calixto's need to turn right would force him to hike numerous steps just to encounter a fretful freefall on the next right turn. Nevertheless, the hilly terrain did not keep him from pursuing his goal. He walked assertively until the inevitable happened. The last turn he made brought him face to face with the nameless woman he had met two days before. They both stopped walking and regarded each other. She started talking and said the vagaries of life were finally coming her way but that she was not clear if that was a good omen. Then she bluntly asked him where he was heading. Calixto took a few seconds to respond, unclear if he wanted to say that he was heading nowhere, that he was merely walking in circles, ever-growing, but circles nonetheless. He also considered saying he was on his way to buying bread. That would have been a paltry lie. Although he considered heading for a bakery at another time in the near future, he was not heading for one that very moment. Once he made up his mind, Calixto explained that he was trying to trace a large spiral by walking in circles of increasing diameter. The woman did not seem surprised, and with her index finger, she traced a spiral in the air just in front of Calixto's face. She mentioned that spirals required a point of axis and asked him what important element was he turning and turning around. Once more, Calixto feared the incisive nature of this woman's questions, her ability to unearth vital information without revealing much of herself. He did not respond. Instead, he invited her to walk along with him. She agreed, and both marched ahead in silence. And just after the first right turn she started to sing a soft melody in a language Calixto could not understand. He was almost certain it was the same language as the words tattooed on her arm. The melody enlaced Calixto's mind, creating a spiral of its own, and for a moment he felt disoriented. When they reached the end of a long block, Calixto, dizzy as he was, attempted to turn left. She held his arm and directed him towards the right instead. She told him that the very important element at the center of the spiral had to be on the right side. When he asked her if she was referring to the aroma of freshly baked bread, she said that she was actually referring to the sound of fresh words.

Is it possible for this woman to know the real importance of words in my life? Bread is just as important, but given both options, she chooses the sound of fresh words. Exactly as I would've done. Just the other day we spoke to each other, but I didn't use words in ways that revealed how much they matter to me. But maybe I did so without knowing. I seem to talk without talking, to share ideas without a clear discourse. And at this very moment, we could be discussing how afraid I'm to say anything to her, how much I fear to become transparent. Even if I'm now silent, we could have spoken to each other at another time, in another place. Then she would know plenty about me. But would it really matter if everything about ourselves had been said before? If that were the case, the words we utter at this very moment would lack freshness; they would be stale and flat. And that's not how it feels. I feel as if we're about to say something surprising to each other, something that would reveal a vast unknown.

After walking for several blocks, making several right turns, and after struggling in his mind with a multitude of questions, Calixto reached a district where the walls of the decrepit buildings stood straight and showed no signs of shame. He did not intend to reach any particular place in this vertical city; he just followed his preconceived trajectory. Not knowing where he was in the large scheme of the spiral, he suddenly stopped walking and asked the woman if she wanted to sit down for a coffee or a glass of wine and talk about things they have not talked about. She agreed, and they sat at an outside terrace completely exposed to the wind, the sun, and the words of the walking crowd. Calixto asked for a glass of Alentejo, and the woman said she wanted the same thing. And this acquiescence disturbed him, for he expected resistance or at least divergence. But he did not allow the sense of distrust to take over, he reigned in all doubtful thoughts and had some of the wine. She did as he had done and both stayed silent for a while, listening to the incessant steps of the crowd that paraded right in front of them. Without a prelude, she asked him if he was proud of the books he had written. This question struck Calixto like a freight train running through the middle of his head. Not only had he not discussed with her the books he had written, but the concept of pride was foreign to him. He wrote because he needed to write, no pride sought, no glory expected. But the fact that she would pose this question so openly and straight disarmed him. There was no answer, and he said so. He drank from his glass, and she emulated him. And trying to avoid further uneasy subjects, Calixto calculated what to ask her in return. He could not contain himself and ventured to ask what her name was. She paused and played with her hair, she bit the nail of her index finger, and looking at him directly she said her name was Leda. She immediately became quiet, silent, and looked away from him. It seemed like she was trying to escape the world. It looked as if she needed to glide away from all contact, physical or mental. She simply stopped existing in front of Calixto and butterflied away. But Calixto could not let her go; he grounded her with another question. He asked if she really considered words essential to her existence, and if so, how did she usually engage with words in her own life. Leda smiled and drank some wine from her glass. Then she looked at her tattoo, those words unknown to Calixto, perhaps looking for an answer in them. And she went on to pronounce the words softly as if layering them one by one, as if those words explained everything about her and about her life. Calixto listened. He felt the words again, the emotion in the words.

Neptune and his trident. The mythical number. Three women, three encounters, three tattoos, and three names that start with the letter "L." This cannot be the product of chance; the world is not that harmless… wicked it is. But what makes it even more disquieting is the fact that the three women intuited that I'm a writer. Could I have precipitated those encounters? Perhaps I inadvertently created the conditions for them to take place. But if that were the case, the number 3 has to be secretly operating inside my mind, subconsciously directing my steps, fabricating falsely fortuitous events. I could consider that probability, but I wouldn't like it if it were true. Chance is beautiful, even dangerous. I need chance in my life. Otherwise, what would be the purpose of walking?

Trying to recapture the sense of serendipity, Calixto attempted to decipher the meaning of the words indelibly imprinted on Leda's forearm. He ventured into the unknown once more. He said the words meant "Love Your Dreams."

To this conjecture, she simply responded with a faint smile that did not confirm nor reject the accuracy of Calixto's guess. And her expression, neutral, would not reveal if Calixto had even approached the themes embedded in the three words. For a moment Calixto considered guessing again, but he stopped himself. He had proposed one meaning, that was sufficient. A second guess would not clarify anything. So he accepted the vagueness of the situation as a clear confirmation that not everything is manipulated by his subconscious mind. Encouraged, Calixto allowed for time to grow on its own, for silence to decide what to do with itself, and for Leda to speak whenever she wanted. He would not pursue any further answers at that moment.

Leda leaned back in her chair and assumed a comfortable position, welcoming the wind and the sun. She asked Calixto if he felt like writing that very moment. He would have loved to say he did, but that would have been another lie. And he feared that she would see through that lie. So Calixto admitted that writing was not an urgent need, that perhaps knowing was more imminent. Leda did not ask him what it was he wanted to know about, as he had expected. Instead, she mentioned that writing should be everyone's need. But before Calixto had time to agree with that statement, she asked him if the center of his spiral felt closer to him that moment. Calixto had forgotten about the smell of freshly baked bread and the sound of fresh words. In her presence, those concerns had disappeared. Perplexed by this realization, he felt a sense of vertigo, as if the very spiral he had conjured was pulling him down into a deep void. He closed his eyes and held on tightly to the wine glass. He waited a few seconds, maybe longer, for the world to feel stable again. Once he felt the ground firm enough, he opened his eyes and found Leda looking directly at him, her expression placid. She asked him if closing his eyes let him walk far into his inner journey. Calixto was not sure how far he had walked, or whether he had walked at all. He may have fallen fathoms into a deep fear, and that kind of emotional journey did not happen in real space. But not ready to admit any sense of uneasiness, he said he had not walked a single centimeter.

The wind started to blow harder. The umbrellas shading the tables rattled. Someone's hat went flying by and disappeared down the street. Calixto was not afraid of the umbrellas or flying objects, but he was afraid the wind would steal his words and never bring them back. And at this moment he needed every single word, so he made sure to keep his mouth closed. He looked at Leda from within his silence, and this must have emphasized the appearance of anguish because Leda asked him if everything was fine. Exposed and vulnerable as he felt, Calixto pretended to be at peace by gazing over the rooftops of the old buildings far out to the magnificently calm Tejo. The river, with silver scars on its back, walked its undulating walk out to the ocean. This vision served to calm Calixto, who stood up and announced he was ready to continue walking and making right turns. Leda said she understood his need, and without further explanations, she got up from the table and followed the wind down the street leaving Calixto standing alone.

As the spiral expanded, the forces at its center began to lose their power. Calixto felt this weakening and stopped walking. He did not want to fall off the spiral for fear of coming unhinged. He considered simply backtracking, circling in the opposite direction towards the point where he had started from. But that would oblige him to walk over the same streets, repeating the walking experience in reverse. That would not elicit fresh words, and he needed them. So he decided to walk in a straight line toward the center of the spiral, skipping over concentric rings, following the centripetal force.

Calixto had not gone too far in his new trajectory when he found himself once more in front of Livraria Mundo. Arriving at that location unexpectedly made him hesitate. He had not planned to be there, but there he was. So he walked inside the old bookstore, hoping to find Lyubochka and her salamander at the sales counter. And that was exactly what he found. This time Lyubochka did not ignore him; to the contrary, she looked directly at him from the moment he went through the door. And before Calixto managed to say anything, she asked him if he had already written about love. Calixto wanted to say he had written volumes and volumes about love since they met the previous day, that he had learned all about her home village in Ukraine, that he had even baked bread. But that was not possible, and she intuited that, for when he did not answer her question, she looked down to her lap and continued reading her book. Calixto felt the weight of the disappointment.

I know about the ancient salamander, the lizard who lives in the fire. It comes out of the fire and extinguishes it. And as quiet as she is, she is just as fiery. What does she expect from me? Or is it me who expects something from myself and she only reminds me of my own expectations? Could she be made of fire? Who knows? All I know is that in her presence I feel uncomfortable. No, not in her presence… in her silence. Her silence cuts through me. The fire of coal is silent, but just as consuming. And she expects me to write about love. Perhaps not about love but about her. But I don't know one nor the other. This is how I fail, by not distinguishing between fire and fear, between love and the object of love. And she knows I should write about that, somehow she knows. But where should I write about love? With the immensity of the Atlantic Ocean on my back? That's what I thought before departing from Nice, that's what brought me to Lisbon. But what brought me to her, to the fire of her expectations? Was it the randomness of my walks? Perhaps my walks are not random at all. And if they were not random, what are the unseen forces pulling on me?

Calixto respected her silence. He wanted to ask her about the book she was reading but thought that would not be prudent. Not when he just failed to respond to her question. He moved about the store and pretended to be looking for a particular book. He shuffled a few titles, read a few random passages, and eventually found a section containing several books by Clarice Lispector. Here he stopped and inspected the copies. They were all in Portuguese. He looked up to Lyubochka who was still immersed in her reading and interrupted her by asking if there were any books by Lispector in English or French. Lyubochka emerged from her reading as if from a dream. She then lifted the book she was reading for Calixto to see. It was a copy of *The Passion According to G.H.* in English translation. Calixto held his breath. He could not comprehend how Lyubochka happened to be reading the very book he would have liked to have found. He proceeded carefully and mentioned that it was precisely that book, *The Passion According to G.H.*, that he was looking for. While caressing the fiery salamander, Lyubochka said that she was happy he found the book he came looking for. And when Calixto asked if he could actually buy that copy, she said he could not buy it because she had not finished reading it yet. And just as simple as that, Lyubochka looked down and continued reading the book.

Unclear as to whose expectations he was not meeting, Calixto considered escaping from the bookstore and continuing his walk down toward the center of the spiral. But the drive to move ahead yielded to the need to solve the intrigue Lyubochka presented. He walked to the sales desk and stood firmly in front of her. There he remained for a few moments, waiting for Lyubochka to acknowledge him. When she eventually stopped reading and looked up at him, he felt a sense of vertigo. In spite of his fear for what might ensue, Calixto persisted in being there, standing, sustaining his equilibrium. Lyubochka started talking and said that somehow the book mirrored him. And she proceeded to quote a phrase she had just read: *"We are creatures that must plunge into the depth in order to breathe there."* Calixto tried to decode what Lispector would have meant by those words. But he was more interested in knowing why Lyubochka thought they had anything to do with him. So he asked her. And he did not get an answer. Instead, Lyubochka went back to reading the book and completely ignored him once more. There were times when Calixto found no words to continue writing. There were other times when he did not find a clear path to follow in his walks. And yet there were other times when he was not clear as to what the universe was preparing for him. This was one of those times.

The only way to comprehend the universe was through words, and Calixto knew that. Nothing could exist in full plenitude until addressed by words. So Calixto turned around and searched the bookshelves for a dictionary. He wanted a sizable volume with the largest number of words. The Cambridge English-Portuguese dictionary caught his attention with its imposing shield, where four lions were flanked by a white cross. He grabbed the dictionary and let the full weight of all the words contained within it fall on the sales desk. The loud thump did not disturb Lyubochka who remained immersed in Lispector's strange and hypnotic prose. Calixto then reached across the desk and took a solitary pen sleeping next to the cash register.

The gesture did not bother Lyubochka a bit. He opened the dictionary and started writing on the white interior of the back cover. He wrote fast, desperately. When he had covered about half of the back cover with his meticulous calligraphy, Lyubochka detached herself from her book and asked him if he was finally writing about love. Calixto stopped in the middle of a sentence and said that he was using words to find the way to the words that might help him understand this moment. That if all the words were contained in this dictionary, a combination of the right ones would certainly shed light on what was about to happen. Lyubochka took a deep breath and seemed pensive. She took the dictionary and turned it in her direction to read what Calixto had written so meticulously. Her expression could not have changed less as she read the text. After returning the dictionary to Calixto, she said that she could not understand the spirit of the characters. She then asked him if he thought the text was capable of breathing.

Words are life. I naturally expect my writing to breathe. But perhaps she's asking something completely different. She wants me to write about love, and love is the meaning of her name. She may be looking for an image of herself in the writing. Or perhaps a living, breathing equivalent of herself. If she's reading Lispector, there must be an existential yearning beating inside of her. Her placid expression could be a mask covering a deep, brutal mystical crisis. Maybe she's the one that must plunge into the depth and breathe there. Regardless, she instigates in me a sense of imbalance, an uneasy feeling that makes me doubt. Yes, I know I need to write books. But that's not where the answer is — not the answer to why an abyss forms in front of me at this moment. I need to write to understand. I need the words to shine their light and lead me to the center of the spiral. They're all there, in the dictionary, the words. A million points of light contained between the covers of that one book. So if the words are not clear to her, if she cannot hear their breath, then I've failed to find the correct ones.

Resolved, Calixto carefully scripted two more sentences on the dictionary's back cover and showed them to Lyubochka. He was certain the words had all the necessary space to breathe. He really meant what the words implied, especially the word "blue." This time Lyubochka broke the surface of the mountain lake and offered him an ample smile. The smile fastened itself to the thin air inside the bookstore and hung there for Calixto to admire. Her response was swift and acute. She said the ocean was there for all to find, that if he traveled west to Adraga, he was certain to find the ocean, a large one, capable of sourcing all the words he needed. She added that water was the essence of all living creatures, including the seagulls, and that to carry an ocean on his back was certainly an advantage if he could tolerate the magnanimous imposition. Calixto did not expect such an apprehending answer. He marveled at the insight Lyubochka revealed. But he felt disappointed that she had not reflected on the color blue, a reference he clearly made on those two sentences. Maybe he left very little room around the word "blue" for Lyubochka to comment. When he imagined writing with the enormous ocean on his back, he imagined an aqueous universe, diaphanous, transparent, and exquisitely blue.

Lyubochka left the sales desk in a rush and went looking for a map of Lisbon. She moved the dictionary to the edge of the desk, without closing it, and opened the map right in front of Calixto. The city, the neighborhoods, and the hills were all there for Calixto to regard. He took some time to become acquainted with the relationship between land and sea. He marveled at the proximity of the ocean and wondered what happened to the waters of the Tejo when they entered the body of the ocean. Did the river waters understand what was happening to them, did they know they were being absorbed? He thought about language and how words from one language had been absorbed by another language throughout the history of the world, over and over again. He wondered if, in the end, the ocean contained all the waters of all the rivers in the world. Likewise, he wondered if one universal language would contain all other languages of the world. But not wanting to destroy the grace of the moment with unbecoming questions, he went back to the color "blue." Calixto pointed to the shores of the Atlantic Ocean on the map and asked Lyubochka if the waters along the shore were blue. She looked at him with the sagacity that had perturbed him earlier and said the ocean had no color of its own, that it only reflected the color of the sky.

Calixto understood what she meant: the essential relativity of all perceptions. And that led him to consider that his need for words was a personal conundrum that would continue to exist in spite of the extensive walking he had done. He also accepted that chance was playing a crafty game on him. But above all, he confronted the possibility that what he considered essential, what he considered utterly obvious, could be questioned. In his genuine depths, Calixto wanted to find the color blue, but such a color would only come forward as a reflection of his own self. So, exposing his vulnerabilities, he asked Lyubochka if she thought the ocean flanking the west of Lisbon would be kind to him. She said he had nothing to fear, that the ocean was simply there.

*****

The path to Adraga was paved with uncertainty. Calixto would need to walk at least nine hours to face the ocean at its rawest. He knew there was no other path, and he needed to forge the path alone. The words of Lyubochka continued to resonate in his mind. The ocean was simply there, there it was. And carrying only the most bare essentials, he ventured west of Lisbon. He imagined what the ocean would look like upon his arrival at Adraga. There would be the color blue, the expansiveness. But he also knew that standing at the shore of the ocean would not be different from standing at the shore of the sea. The blue body of the Mediterranean would resemble the Atlantic Ocean. But perhaps what resided in the horizon beyond the line between the two blues was completely different. That was not a tangible element; it only existed in the realm of the mind. For Calixto, beyond had yet to happen. He was searching for a vision of beauty, and a new language, the one he knew had to exist.

Along the long road to Adraga, Calixto saw people engaged in needs so different from his own. Children went to school, office workers went into their tombs, and dogs looked for inviting posts. The world turned in so many different ways. Those realities meant nothing to him at that point, he knew they had a place in the world, and he also knew they would continue to exist independent of him. So he carried forward, walking at a pace that would bring him to the ocean in the late afternoon. But what he could not have predicted was to come across the image of a woman who resembled Lulu walking toward him. Upon such sighting, he went under an awning on the side of the street and remained motionless. From that vantage point he observed the figure of Lulu, or someone who looked like her, move past him and disappear through a side street. He had encountered a similar image while sitting at Praça do Rossio, and now he wondered if this was the same image or a similar sensation. He was not prepared to make the distinction between a real image or a sensation, so he treated the experience as if it was the very image of Lulu. But by the time he decided to follow her, the image, or the sensation, whatever that was, had already vanished.

Undeterred, Calixto continued his long walk. He tried to follow long, uninterrupted lines; he avoided turning right or left; he kept his gaze ahead and followed the distant smell of salty water. Ahead of him was the ocean, and perhaps, the words he needed. And the pull of those words was so hard that Calixto did not realize the passage of time, the passage of distance. He walked, and he walked some more. And by the time the sun was calming itself down, Calixto had arrived at a promontory from where he could see the horizon opening up in front of him. He regarded the blue, the expansiveness. He readied himself for a new language.

Calixto approached the ocean. He felt its cold and raw nature, and its yearning to extend itself out west, far beyond where he had ever ventured. The roar of the ocean was magnanimous, and Calixto knew that words could be sourced from that immense volume of sound. So there he stood, at the shore, tired from walking all day, but ecstatic to be in the presence of such magnificence. He closed his eyes and took a deep breath. The salty air flooded his lungs, and his mind felt as if he was part of something larger than himself. He felt a sense of belonging as if all beings were connected to each other by means of the waters circling the world. And that oceanic sense of connectedness gave him hope. Perhaps his random encounters with men and women along his extended walks had a sense and a meaning after all.

Soon the sun turned red, and Calixto started walking back to the nearby village of Almoçageme to find a place to sleep. It was a short stretch but the long day started to weigh him down. Had the ocean not infused him with new energy, he would have collapsed on the sandy beach. Once he reached the village, Calixto came across a *quinta* that seemed welcoming. He went inside and asked the host if they had a quiet room with an open view. The host said he had the perfect room for him on the top floor, overlooking the horizon, with a distant view of the ocean. Calixto accompanied the host to take a look at the room and found it utterly appropriate for his needs. He then agreed to stay there for five days, perfectly knowing that five days would not be enough to accomplish much in terms of language. Once the host left, he collapsed on the bed and abandoned himself to recumbent relaxation. The morning would arise with a brand new offering, or so Calixto expected. But somehow, the hours between night and morning needed to be endured. The night arrived at once and swallowed him complete. But as soon as he went into REM sleep, his dreams took flight. He saw himself standing in front of a large crowd in an amphitheater, dressed like an ancient actor, delivering phrases by Euripides: "Some shrewd and intelligent man invented fear of the gods for mortals, so the wicked would have something to fear... concealing the truth with a false account." He heard the crowd applaud. He then declared other phrases, elucidating, even brilliant, and he felt understood. His capacity to transmit his thought process by means of words made him feel accomplished in his dreams. But when the night came to an end, in the impossible morning hours, the most despicable moment of the sleep cycle, Calixto woke up feeling as if he was betrayed. He had spoken the words of the heroes in his dreams, but the erratic day showed a burning face certain to challenge him, to reverse his accomplishment.

Calixto left behind his bed and his doubts and went to open the window in his room. The light rushed to meet him, a blue light. And far beyond the hills, a sliver of ocean saluted him. He felt a sense of belonging as if he was where he needed to be at this very moment in his life. And knowing that such a feeling could easily prove temporary, he prepared himself to walk to the beach to confront the ocean, the words, and the unknown.

At the breakfast room, the host asked Calixto if he wanted a basket of croissants. He said he preferred bread, any kind of bread as long as it was fresh. The host then asked him if he wanted coffee or tea. Calixto said he preferred a good glass of Douro. The host said he understood and brought him the glass of wine. He then asked Calixto what had brought him to Adraga. Calixto pondered for a while, he knew the essential forces that brought him there, but he had doubts about those other forces that lay buried deep in his unconscious mind. Those were the forces he feared the most. But after a moment of consideration, he said that words had brought him there. The host looked at him and made a grimace that he could not decipher. Calixto could have said that the ocean brought him there. But in reality, the ocean was what he found after getting there. The words, or the search for words, was the true force behind his long walk from Lisbon. But explaining this to the host was not what he intended. So he simply drank the wine, all at once, and took to the road to follow the salty air.

Calixto approached the ocean slowly. He saw how the horizon grew blue in front of him. He noticed how the sound of the waves overtook all other sounds. He observed how the limit of his visual field expanded until vanishing completely. And far away he saw that line between the two blues, the line he could not reach unless he walked on water. From that spot, he walked down the beach until finding a rock where he could sit down and begin the labor of words. He was exactly where he wanted to be, so he dove into the language.

Sometimes, words came to Calixto as blue words, perhaps wet and salty. Other times words bounced on the surface of the ocean, traveling from wave crest to wave crest, finally arriving at him entirely dry. Other words just floated in the air, at the whim of the winds, erratic in their behavior. Calixto appreciated the unpredictable words, but at the same time, he needed certain consistency. Capturing the various words proved a challenging task. He tried to compose sentences that contained an elegant mixture of the various word sources, but he failed. When he wanted salty words, they were not available. When he needed a dry word, a wet one would land on his lap. When he aimed at channeling the whimsical nature of the windy words, they flew around him in spirals making it impossible for him to grab a single one. He then waited for the silvery words, those that grew from the underside of the waves when caught by the oblique sunlight. Those words traveled faster than any other words; they were fleeing the pressure between water and light; they were blinding. Calixto caught a couple of those silvery words and felt lucky. He waited and held onto some of the wet and dry words.

Not having an immediate obligation other than creating and advancing his prose, he continued this exercise until he had gathered a significant number of words. He then tried to construct phrases with all the words he had assembled. The essential purpose was to create innovative prose, or so he thought. But then he thought about Lyubochka who had directed him west. He thought about Leda and the absence of words to describe her absence. And he thought about Lulu and her uncertain silhouette. Calixto could not dismiss the impact those three women had on him. He then understood that real writing would not take place until he could verbalize what those experiences represented.

The sun stepped on him, and the winds pushed him around. Calixto felt the force of the elements and realized he could not fight against them either. So he offered his skin to the sun and his hair to the wind. He allowed for anything existing outside of his skin to have its way with him. Inside, however, he tried to establish some control. He began by thinking about Lulu and admitting he could not effectively grasp her image. A fleeting image had no handles. He considered Leda and accepted the fluid nature of her soul, and in so being, her unsubstantial quality. As for Lyubochka, he felt a genuine admiration for her calm demeanor and her intuitive nature. The three of them could exist at the same time inside his mind; they just needed to find their own private corner. So, once at peace with the divergent feelings those three women elicited, Calixto felt at ease with himself, relieved, free to unleash his creative power.

The hours marched in front of Calixto without disturbing him. Absorbed in his writing, he ignored their passage. He also ignored the arrival of several people who came to share the beach with him. From time to time he would look up from his writing and watch people frolicking on the sand and bathing in the ocean. For him, they did not exist as people; they were entities that turned into a blue substance that blended with the horizon. Everything he saw or heard existed only for a fraction of a second before joining the magnificent body of water extending in front of him. And in such a state he remained until the moment a hand landed on his left shoulder. Calixto turned and saw a wrinkled hand pressing him down, but when he looked up to find out who that hand belonged to, the sun blinded him. He then stood up, and when his eyes adjusted to the new light, he found himself in front of the deeply carved face of the old man he had met at the bookstore. He could not imagine how the old man found him on this remote beach. But there he was, standing in front of him, not saying a single word, impassive, as if he had been there for ages. Calixto felt the same uneasy feeling as when he sat in front of the old man at his store.

A strange nakedness. And when he was about to react, to say something, the old man beat him to the point and asked him if he had made advances in filling the void. Calixto did not answer the question. And somehow the old man had not expected an answer because at once he showed Calixto the copy of his own book, *No Somos Pero Somos*, and told him he was enjoying it tremendously. When Calixto asked him what was he doing in Adraga, the old man said he had come to talk to him about the book and the void. And when

Calixto asked him how did he manage to find him in Adraga, the old man reminded him that he had worked for the resistance. The old man then sat on the rock next to the one where Calixto was sitting and proceeded to read *No Somos Pero Somos* in silence.

The ocean behaved as if nothing had happened. It remained placid in its immensity. And Calixto found that comforting. He then sat down in front of the old man and continued to write. He was creating new prose at the same time the old man was consuming prose he had created in the past. Calixto felt as if they were both on the same plane, like a Möbius strip, a cycle twisted on itself with no beginning or end. And sharing a common plane with the old man made Calixto wonder what his name would be. So he asked the old man what his name was. The old man looked at him, and clearly puzzled said his name was of no importance. Then Calixto asked again how did he want to be called. The old man took pause, he regarded the ocean as if something would emerge from it, and then asked Calixto to call him Theo.

When the afternoon arrived, it found the two men still sitting in front of each other. They had not spoken since the morning. And it was not until Calixto said he had nothing more to write, that Theo said he had nothing more to read. Then they stood up and agreed to walk back to Almoçageme to find something to eat.

*****

The walk back to Almoçageme turned into a crawl. Calixto had to slow his pace so that Theo could keep up with him. The old man did not seem out of breath, but his steps were significantly shorter than those of Calixto. In addition, at every turn of the road, Theo would look behind him and around him, as if he were afraid of being followed. Calixto asked him if there was something wrong and Theo responded that nothing was wrong, that everything seemed right, as far as he could ascertain. They eventually made it to the *quinta* where Calixto was staying. Theo greeted the host in the most familiar way, and after exchanging a few words in Portuguese, they were seated at a table in a quiet corner. The host brought a bottle of Douro and poured two glasses. He then asked if they were interested in dining at once. Calixto indicated he was ready, but Theo asked the host to wait a little longer because he had to discuss a serious matter before dinner. This request surprised Calixto. He could not imagine what serious matter Theo intended to discuss with him.

After toasting and drinking half of his glass of wine, Theo told Calixto that everything he had read in *No Somos Pero Somos* was a lie. Calixto accepted the premise but pointed out that he only wrote fictional lies, not real ones. He was not interested in the real lies people tell; those were better dealt with in real life. He was more interested in the creation of lies intended to exist within a fictional world. Theo listened attentively to the explanation. He remained quiet and drank some more of the wine. Then he asked Calixto if those lies, the fictional ones, would not necessarily get closer and closer to reality. He thought that was the real danger, that one could inadvertently breach the line between fiction and reality. He then added that approaching that line from the fictional side would be a reversal from the direction in which writers commonly travel. For Calixto, whether that porous line was breached coming from the real or the fictional side had no importance, and he said so. Before continuing their conversation, Theo insisted on Calixto drinking some more of the wine. He said both of them had to be equally influenced. Calixto obeyed. Then Theo spoke about the need to create false appearances during the times of Salazar, how the resistance had taught him to pretend, how nothing was what it seemed to be. He said that each person in the resistance was a novel. Calixto imagined the unbearable experiences Theo had endured. He also understood that a reader like Theo would read a novel in a completely different manner from another reader whose life did not seem like a novel itself. This time Calixto was the one who remained quiet and drank some of the wine. Theo faced him, a hard face he had, and murmured something Calixto did not understand.

The host brought a few olives and a basket of bread to their table. He asked again if they were ready to order. Theo presented him with his hard face, and the host understood to leave them alone for the moment. When Calixto reached for a piece of bread, Theo was quick to hold his hand, preventing him from grabbing anything. He let go of Calixto's hand and said that instincts could often betray the man, that we should not necessarily do what we felt like doing. In his opinion, reigning in one's instincts was not deceitful but protective. Calixto mentioned that he saw no need to protect himself in such a manner. A subtle smirk broke the hardness of Theo's face. And then he asked Calixto if he really had the words he needed to write his new book.

Do I really have the words I need? And why does he question that? In front of the ocean, I feel overwhelmed by words; there's no shortage of them. He was there; he saw me writing. But maybe what the old man senses is the void, that void Lispector wrote about. And these questions must be important for him since he came all the way from Lisbon to find me. I wonder what I represent for him. Perhaps a friend lost or murdered during the times of Salazar. Maybe I look like his son. Maybe he's looking for words himself. Or maybe his own void is larger than mine. I don't know. But he seemed at ease reading while I was writing. I must admit I also felt at ease. We both shared the same plane, the plane of language. I believe we were both creating at the same time. I was forging phrases while he was deciphering them. He created his own version of my book. Every text is reinvented when read. Perhaps the real creative communion happens when a writer writes while his writing is being read simultaneously.

So Calixto said that even if the words became scarce, he had conceived of a way to procure them. And he said this in such a convincing fashion that Theo did not see the need to question him, he just accepted the statement. Calixto then grabbed the piece of bread he was longing for and consumed it with great delight while Theo watched him attentively and drank still more wine. With a quick gesture, Theo summoned the host, and they finally ordered their meal. By the time the food arrived at the table the bottle of wine was completely empty. Theo asked for another bottle. They ate in complete silence, facing each other, sharing words that existed only in their minds, words that had yet to be written or read. When the meal was over, the night had descended in its entirety, and the two men were still sitting in front of each other. They were talking without saying a single word.

Eventually, Theo stood up and said he had to return to Lisbon, that he needed to open the shop in the morning because people deserved open access to books. He explained that the fact the current government was not a repressive one did not guarantee that other forces dissuaded people from reading good literature. For him, the most powerful force was undirected and purposeless freedom because it gave people more opportunities than they could handle. People were bound to sink into the pit of the lowest common denominator, he thought. Calixto noticed how Theo's hands started to shake, and his face became even harder. He could not tell if it was the alcohol that made him tremulous or his grave concern for the infirm situation of the reading public. And as Theo started walking away from the *quinta*, Calixto realized he had left the copy of *No Somos Pero Somos* on top of the table. He picked up the book and ran after Theo. When he attempted to give him the book, Theo said it did not make any sense for him to keep the book. Yes, he had not finished reading it, but he would only continue to read the book in Calixto's presence and only if Calixto were to be writing at the same time right in front of him. Then he just left.

Back in his room Calixto sat at the edge of his bed and looked out the window. He tried to find the reflection of the moon on the surface of the ocean. But the night insisted on being dark and offered no light whatsoever. Then he tried to listen for the waves. He thought he heard them, but that would have been impossible. He listened more attentively to all the sounds the night brought to the window. There were a few scattered words he could not understand. Perhaps the host was talking to someone. He then opened his own book, *No Somos Pero Somos*, and read random sentences. He tried to imagine how those words sounded inside Theo's mind. Did the words have the same timbre, cadence, and melancholic character of his own voice, his Calixto's voice? Or, most likely, did Theo hear his own personal voice, his Theo's voice, as if he himself had written the words down and was now talking to himself? Theo had only started reading the book after they had met, after having the opportunity to hear each other's voice. So he supposed that Theo read *No Somos Pero Somos* having his voice, Calixto's voice, inside his mind. This was an uneasy feeling because Calixto did not want to exist as a voice in other people's mind. But he could not stop wondering what voice would readers hear inside their minds when they had never met the author and heard his or her real voice. Readers had to invent a voice, any voice that seemed appropriate, he considered. But that left much to the vagaries of chance. Perhaps, he thought, readers hear versions of their own voices. They match their own joy with the joy of the book, pain with pain, and fear with fear in an ever-changing sequence of emotions dictated by the text. Calixto continued reading passages from his own book until the night quieted everything down and his mind fell asleep.

*****

The morning arrived with urgency. The clear light doused Calixto with such audacity that he had no other

option but to get up at once and consider the day. He re-
called the events that had transpired the previous night.
He thought about Theo and his capacity to behave as a dop-
pelgänger, a reflection of his own needs. He would have
liked to talk to him that very morning before setting out
for the new unknown. But Theo was probably in Lisbon
opening his bookstore, taking care of the needs of anonymous readers. So Calixto grabbed the copy of *No Somos
Pero Somos* and confronted the day on his own. He started walking towards Adraga, hoping to meet the vast ocean
face-to-face once more. But then, by pure chance, his feet
struck an abandoned path that led away from the beach
instead of toward it. He stopped walking at once and stood
calmly on the desolate path. He accepted the unexpected
desires of a random morning, but he still wanted to return
to the beach where he hoped to find a new stream of words.
So he stood there, motionless, waiting for the competing
drives to settle down. Once his mind found some peace, he
corrected his course and headed toward the ocean. He then
walked at a steady rate until the blue grew immense right
in front of him.

Calixto searched for the same rock where he had sat the
previous day. That vantage point had provided a clear angle
to watch the ocean and source the words he needed. He
found it without much effort and sat down immediately to
prepare himself for the vagaries of a day of prose. But as
he started to write, he felt an intense urge to move closer
to the edge of the surf and walk along the beach. He could
walk north towards a promontory where the rocks and the
ocean met. The wind maneuvering around the rocks was
certain to be strong there, salty. That wind would likely

produce sounds, and on that account, create words he had yet considered. He could use those words during his writing day to give his prose the fugitive sense of falling, spiraling, burning. He could then walk back under the sun to his sitting rock, carrying the bounty of words in his mind, and then continue writing. Convinced, Calixto set out to meet the edge of the surf. As he reached the unquiet water, the surf charged him with an impetus he had not expected, only to retreat quickly, not because of cowardice, but because the ocean pulled back on it. He stepped forward and backward in an attempt to remain at the very edge of the white surf. And to this end, he stepped over hard sand and quicksand in an insane rhythm that tested his balance. He soon realized this back and forth movement prevented him from walking north across the beach to the rocky promontory where he expected to find the shimmering words. So he walked away from the edge of the surf and watched its movement from the safety of hard sand. Then a strong wind blew from the ocean, and the surf lost its white head. He felt sorry for the surf, so incessant and so feeble.

Once at the north end of the beach, Calixto climbed the dark rocks and took a good look at the expansive ocean in front of him, a body so vast he felt compelled to join it. He grabbed the copy of *No Somos Pero Somos* that Theo had left behind and hurled it into the brave waters. He gave his words to the ocean. His writer's body was now inside the body of the ocean. He then grabbed on to a hard rock and closed his eyes. He focused on listening to the wind, to the swirling words. Soon he realized how the position of his head changed the way the wind spoke to him. If he faced the wind straight on, both ears equally captured the words rushing by. This proved to be confusing. But if he turned his head ninety degrees to the right or to the left, exposing only one ear to the wind at a time, he had a better chance to listen to the words. So Calixto held onto the rock while oscillating his head from one side to the other as if saying "no" to the wind, but in reality, accepting all the words the wind had to offer.

Drunk on words, Calixto walked back to the spot where he had planned to write until dusk. All the relevant forces coalesced to catapult him forward into daring prose. And he started writing and looking for the edge, the line at the verge of a precipice, a precipice that contained nothing but pure bliss. And the words were flying, and the images were dawning, and the unconscious was humming, all as it ought to be when he saw the silhouette of a woman walking toward him from where the sun was shining. He could not distinguish who it was when looking into the harsh sunlight. But when the silhouette came close enough to block the sunlight completely, Calixto found himself facing Lyubochka. She did not say anything to Calixto; she simply sat down next to him and looked out to the ocean. Then, in the most casual tone, Lyubochka asked him if he had found what he came looking for. Calixto was looking for many things, some of which he was not even aware he was looking for. And he knew that, the blurry line between the known and the unknown. So all he managed to say was that he had found the ocean just as she had suggested.

Calixto continued writing with the same impetus as before. Now, however, he had a witness. Sitting next to him, Lyubochka observed as he wrote every single word. She made no comments or remarks, nor did she react to the meaning of the words. But she watched attentively as he wrote and wrote. Neither of them had proposed this arrangement, but they did not fight it either. And this communion continued for a while until the moment when Calixto stopped writing abruptly. He seemed dubitative, unsure what to write next. He waited for a few minutes, but nothing occurred to him. He then looked far into the horizon hoping to find vagabond words somewhere out there, between the ocean and the sky. And as he regarded the grand openness, so did Lyubochka. He wondered if she was also looking for elusive words or if she just wanted to share that uncertain moment. He decided to hold his gaze on the horizon for a moment longer. Not only because he had not found what to write next, but to see if Lyubochka would accompany him in the prolonged effort. And she did. She placidly sustained her gaze, unperturbed by the sun or the seagulls. The ocean stretched as far as anyone could see and it did not care that it was being watched by people on the shore. It continued to undulate, to grow small wavelets on its back, to reflect the sun, to allow currents in the deep of its belly, and to send the surf out to the beach. Lyubochka was aware of the ocean's indifference. So she interrupted the long period of contemplation and asked Calixto if he knew the meaning of every word he had written that day. He responded that every word had a meaning but that he did not always know what that meaning was. Then she said she did not understand the ocean either.

For a moment Calixto considered asking what led her all the way from Lisbon to Adraga. But afraid of the potential answer, he withheld the question. Instead, he proposed his own answer. He told Lyubochka there was no need for her to come all the way to Adraga to confirm the ocean was, in fact, just here; that she had made the trip because she felt bored at the bookstore and needed the dynamic force of the ocean to bring life to her day. She smiled but did not respond to his statement. He then proposed to continue with their writing. She quickly remarked that the one writing was him, that she was only an observer. Calixto wanted to disagree, but he did not. So he stopped looking at the horizon and concentrated on trying to write in front of Lyubochka, his witness. By that time, the sun had moved further to the west, and the rays came at an obtuse angle, bouncing off the surface of the ocean and reaching straight into his eyes. This made writing a little more difficult for he needed to squint or block the sunlight with his hand. Lyubochka did not seem bothered at all; she just closed her eyes and let the sunlight bathe her face and the salamander on her neck. He admired her natural peace, how her face became a canvas for the drawings of light and wind. But determined to accomplish his mission, Calixto continued to write in silence, under the sun, in front of the ocean.

Who found whom? I just wonder. I walked into her store on my own accord. She said the ocean was just here. I walked west to Adraga because I wanted to write at the edge. Or, perhaps I walked west to Adraga hoping to find her here, even if that would have been unlikely. If that were indeed the thought process that led me to this beach, I would have to admit I wasn't aware of it. But the truth is that here she is and here I am. Then I wonder if my walking is driven by the need to write or the need to encounter elusive souls that I can barely understand. And there was Theo. Did I come here looking for him as well? I don't think I did but didn't I? And both of these esoteric people interact with my writing in strange ways. They seem to foster the prose, or better yet, exist alongside the prose. So I wonder if writers should write alone, or if we are supposed to write in the company of those who seem to know something about us that we've yet to understand. I fear the answer to that question. For the moment there's the ocean, there's the intense blue, there's the wind, there's the placidity of Lyubochka's face. For the moment I exist as a writer.

Calixto wrote with intensity. From time to time he looked out to the horizon. Other times he gazed at Lyubochka discretely, as if he was not interested in her, pretending he did not care what she was doing. He did care, and she knew he did. But both continued to do what they were doing. Then came the moment that Calixto had secretly feared and had not yet accepted. Lyubochka stood up and said she needed to return to Lisbon. He regarded her, broken inside but firm on the exterior. He said he was not finished writing for the day. She looked straight at him and produced a smile he had never seen before on anyone. And with the same facility with which she arrived, she left. Calixto considered running after her and asking if she could stay until his writing was finished. But he soon realized the baseness of this request. His writing belonged to him, all of it, and no other person could permanently influence it. These fleeting experiences could affect his writing temporarily, yes, but the influence would only be circumscribed to a specific moment and place. And holding onto that line of thought, he watched as Lyubochka walked along the beach until she made a right turn and disappeared from his view.

Calixto felt alone at that moment. Yes, he had come to Adraga alone, but the fact that he felt lonely indicated that something had happened to worsen his condition. A man who walks alone is a man who walks alone. A man who walks alone, and then interacts with people in ways that change the man, is a man who is no longer walking alone. So he wondered if meeting strangers were somehow eroding his condition as a lonesome walker. Even when he had never considered himself as a lonesome walker, he suspected that he was, to some extent, a loner. But walking entailed moving from one place to another, a displacement. And inherent in displacement one found loneliness. But displacement also produced chance encounters with souls he had never known before. Would not those new encounters annihilate the sense of loneliness? Perhaps, but if he felt a sense of affiliation with a new encounter, and the new affiliation would, all of a sudden, come to an end, would not that lead once more to essential loneliness? Calixto did not have an answer to those questions. He was battling the strong sentiment of loneliness after Lyubochka's departure, and at the same time, he was facing the strong urge to continue writing in front of the ocean. Then he thought of all those other writers that had come before him, all of those who had persevered in spite of essential doubts. And pacifying his thought process, he looked out to the horizon, regarding once more the line between the two blues, and he wrote a few more words.

At the end of the day, when he felt completely drained of words, Calixto decided to enjoy the product of his hard labor. He regarded the vastness of his writing, the countless paragraphs and innumerable words he had woven in the last two days. He then attempted to read a few passages to connect with the feeling of the story. But he found the sentences made no sense. He turned one page after another; he tried to understand what he had written so arduously. And once again, the text scurried through the crevices of his mind as water between his fingers. Nothing meaningful remained, only the loneliness.

*****

He walked back to Lisbon, a defeated soldier with a deep vagueness in his soul. Calixto knew the future in Lisbon already existed ahead of him. He knew about the inevitability of arriving in the old city, of looking for fresh bread. But what he could not fathom was how to recover his writing and his sense of being. Was he supposed to avoid people to sustain his loneliness, or was he obligated to search for new encounters with unknown people in the unknown streets of Lisbon? This was not clear to him when he checked back into the hotel. And for that reason, he decided to do nothing and allow for the passage of time to bring clarity. Although he was tired from the long walk back from Adraga, he could not fall asleep. He sat in silence and meditated as the day took all its time to pass by.

Several centuries later, or so it seemed, Calixto realized the passage of time was not providing any clarity. So, in spite of feeling the weight of lead pulling him down, he walked out into the street hoping for an epiphany. He walked up and down and around the city blocks. He avoided making eye contact with strangers for fear of unintended consequences. He just moved his body from one place to another. For a moment he considered whirling, like the Sufi Dervishes, to search for the source of all perfection. But he could never sustain such intensity. Finally, in the middle of a tiresome street, he sat on the curb and watched the passersby. He imagined the infinity of thoughts those other walkers had in their minds, their fears, their dilemmas. And somehow, he identified with them. A sense of collective nihilism dawned on him. Not wanting to roll down the street like a worthless pebble, Calixto picked himself up and tried to walk with his head up and his gaze forward. And that was when he saw once more the image of a woman who resembled Lulu walking about 50 meters ahead of him. The woman was walking rather fast, so Calixto accelerated his pace to try to get a better glimpse. He was not sure that it was Lulu, but the resemblance was significant enough not to be ignored. Although he tried, he could not keep up with her speed. He walked as fast as his tired body permitted, trying to get a glimpse of her right ankle and the three red stars, but the woman still gained distance on him until finally disappearing at the top of a hilly street.

Resolved that no resolution would be had that day, Calixto made his way back to the hotel. He refused to think he was retreating from the world, from the ubiquitous uncertainty. He recognized his arrival in Lisbon proposed no other expectations than to write copiously and to be in the vicinity of the ocean. He had met both of those expectations. So the sense of uneasiness he felt that moment had to be the result of his failure in Adraga. Perhaps, he thought, those chance encounters had altered the delicate mechanism of his inner peace, perhaps the waters were not that still anymore.

Once in bed, dreaming about dreaming, but in reality, just lying down with his eyes open, Calixto watched the street lights coming through the window and splashing against the wall of the hotel room. The long day was over but, he feared what the next day would bring. He imagined waking up in the morning with a clear mind and no trace of apprehension. But he also worried he would stare into an abysmal morning. And after switching between hopeful thoughts and aberrant fears, Calixto finally concluded that the morning would arrive regardless of his expectations. So he abandoned himself to the flow of the passing minutes, to the flickering street lights reflected on the wall, and he fell asleep.

The morning did arrive as Calixto had expected. He prepared himself for the arduous work of being a writer assailed by uncomfortable doubts he could not even name. He looked out the window to confirm that the world was the same as he last saw it the night before. And he was pleased to see that nothing had changed, just the angle of the sun rays. He was determined to exist on this day as a *tabula rasa*, to allow the events, the people, and the words to find him supple, agreeable. He wanted this day to be different. To find a new footing on the sidewalks, he changed his typical walking shoes. And he did not pack his laptop computer, settling instead for a simple pad and pen. The idea was to enter this day completely unencumbered.

The first thing to impact Calixto as he ventured onto the narrow streets of the Alfama, was the sensation that his memory had abandoned him. For a moment he doubted he was a writer because he could not really remember what he had written before. He paused, he reflected, he took several deep breaths and delicately, at the speed of a falling feather, the memory of having written *No Somos Pero Somos* landed in his apprehensive mind. This seemed a difficult way to be a *tabula rasa.* Did being supple and agreeable require having no foundation, no history? Unable to entertain those questions in the early morning, Calixto forged ahead on his walk. The sole of his feet palpated the cobblestones and the crevices on the sidewalks. He glided along the streets as if he belonged in that old part of town. And he allowed all impressions to impact him, olfactory, visual, tactile, all of them. And he felt light.

Calixto then tried to remember what the central theme was of *No Somos Pero Somos.* Nothing came to his mind, just a white vacuum. He considered the title and tried to remember what the book was about. The vacuum blossomed. Then he realized the symmetry in the words composing the title. But this did not offer any clues into the meaning of the book. He resisted caving into the sensation that his past had died. Perhaps, he thought, to find new words and carve new prose, one needed to forget all the words used in the past and all the phrases previously composed. If the writing past was eviscerated, perhaps, a true *tabula rasa* could be had. But Calixto could not accept the destructive nature of such a construct. He wanted to write at the edge; he wanted to create fresh language. But he was not interested in destructing previous creations. After all, Michelangelo did not destroy his David before painting the Sistine Chapel. So he suspended all analytical thinking and abandoned himself to feeling and experiencing what the day had to offer.

The sun took refuge behind a low layer of clouds. He could still see the clear yellow disc, but not strong enough to make him blink. He accepted the tepid sun. He then heard singing coming from far away, fado perhaps, and he accepted not knowing what the song wanted to convey. Then he captured the smell of freshly baked bread. He knew this was inevitable, that at some point in his walking trajectory the smell of life would strike him. But what he was not expecting was to come face-to-face, once again, with Leda. And that was exactly what happened when he turned a corner in pursuit of the smell of life. Leda was walking up the street with a fresh baguette under her arm. Calixto stopped in his tracks and waited for Leda to approach him, not sure exactly what to say or do. Leda kept walking up the street until she reached him. She then excused herself, went past him, and continued walking up the street. When Calixto saw her walking away, he went after her. He was following the unknown, he was following life, or perhaps he was following the concept of his own self as reflected by the tranquil waters of a placid lake.

Once Calixto caught up with Leda, he asked her if she knew where she was going. She said she knew just as much as he did, no more, no less. He then said that his day was not yet determined, that he was open to everything and anything, that he had no clear idea of his destination. Leda congratulated him. And as they had done before, they walked next to each other for a while. Once they reached a small square flanked by a building clad in blue tiles where the Tejo could be seen in the distance, Leda asked him if he intended to be a writer that day. Calixto responded that he intended to be a writer every single day but that life, somehow, managed to insert itself in the middle and derail his intentions. Leda said that life struck everyone every day. He knew she was correct, so he did not counter her assertion. He wanted that day to be nubile, clean. So he asked her if she would suggest a few words to ignite his writing day. Leda heard him and offered him a very clean, unencumbered smile. She then took a piece of her baguette and savored it as if she was savoring life. Calixto wanted to share that bread; he also wanted to hear any words Leda would suggest. But all she offered him were the waters of a tranquil lake.

Calixto looked over the building roofs, far to the west, to the river that moved parsimoniously. The Tejo did not care about his day. The universe clearly did not care about his day either. So he then wondered why would Leda care about his day or his writing. Perhaps she did, perhaps she needed to stumble across him on a random street to find meaning in her own day. But if she needed him as much as he needed her, in that *tabula rasa* of a day, she was not revealing such need. So Calixto took the risk to ask again about those words tattooed on her arm. Leda heard his inquiry and regarded him for a while. She ate another piece of bread with natural detachment. She also looked out to the Tejo and seemed to read its waters. And gracefully, speaking as if a morning mist came out of her mouth, she pronounced the words tattooed on her arm and she told Calixto those were the words he was looking for.

Calixto fell deep inside of himself. He attempted to unravel the meaning of those words to no avail. He tried to relate the sound of Leda's words to the sound of other words known to him. And nothing came close but the cacophony of a garbled phrase. He knew the words were meaningful to her, but he could not make any sense of them. Leda had offered him a spark that did not light any fire. Ashamed, Calixto admitted he did not understand the words, but that he believed they were rather important to her. Leda listened to him, and her face glowed under the tepid sun. She then admitted the words represented the myth of who she thought she was, and because he seemed to be on some kind of quest, she thought the words would be useful to him as well. That kindness comforted Calixto even though he remained in virtual darkness about Leda and the words tattooed on her arm. He was unclear what to expect from her; he did not know if to continue questioning her, follow her, or just turn around and walk away. But respecting his plan to be open to everything that day, Calixto took Leda's arm and read the unintelligible words at loud mimicking her pronunciation. He then thanked her for the offer.

Calixto then focused on the three-story building clad in blue and white tiles. He realized the tiles covered the entire façade. On further observation, he discovered the tiles depicted a naval battle. There were ships, sailors, waves, swords, cannons, even sea monsters, all entangled in the most intricate battle. He could not recognize the forces depicted, what king, what country. But what caught his attention was a three-headed sea monster devouring an unfortunate sailor. It was brutal. The sailor stood no chance against the creature. And he could not help but think about the number 3 and its many iterations. Today, immortalized on the façade of a three-story building, a three-headed creature was massacring a powerless sailor. And he could conceive that if the story continued if the tiles could tell what happened next, the monster would have carried on his carnage until stopped by a cannonball. Cutting one head out of three would not have been enough to stop him. He needed to be struck directly in the heart.

He then asked Leda if she saw anything peculiar in the story illustrated by the blue tiles. With a distracted air, Leda regarded the tiles. She spent a long time looking while sustaining a pleasant smile on her face. Her eyes traversed the façade without focusing on any particular detail. She appeared to be peacefully drinking in the story. When she finished, she told Calixto that the story was probably a lie, that reality could never look that way. But that as an interpretation of how people feel when vulnerable seemed rather accurate. She then added that being eaten by a three-headed monster seemed particularly cruel. Calixto asked her if it would have been any better if the monster had only one head. Leda smiled and did not answer his question; instead, she asked him if he was going to write about sea monsters. He had not intended to write about monsters of any kind, but accepting this day as a *tabula rasa*, he accepted such possibility but clarified that the real monsters, the ones that could bite your head off, were within yourself. Leda looked at him peacefully, and before she could utter a single word, Calixto went ahead and said he knew what she was thinking, that she would ask him what his inner monsters were. Leda smiled again and explained that since he had posed the question himself, it was up to him to answer it. Calixto then fell deeper inside himself. Unable to answer clearly, he ventured to write the words Leda had offered him, those tattooed on her arm. He tried to write them phonetically, as she had pronounced them. He looked up to the sky and waited for the air to bring back the sound of the words. Once he connected with the sounds, he wrote three words on the pad. He took a deep breath, looked at the blue tiles, and handed the pad to Leda. She donned a pure smile.

And without saying anything else, Leda moved on with her life. She walked away from Calixto, down the street with her baguette under her arm. She did not look back even once. Calixto felt like shouting those three words so she would perhaps stop walking. But he did not do that. He simply watched as she walked down the street and became a fluttering leaf in the river of people. He had not expected Leda to appear in his life that day, but that being a day where anything could have happened, he was not surprised that she came and left as she did. Or, at least, that was what he wanted to believe.

Look at the battle portrayed on the façade of that building. Who initiated the aggression, what were the circumstances, who was the victor? I wonder if the three-headed monster took one side over the other, or was the monster operating on its own, eating away unanimously. That monster is the very representation of evil. It inserts itself in the middle of a naval battle as if it belonged there. Can evil exist as a force of its own, independent from those who seem to sponsor it or to suffer from it? Does evil take sides? Maybe evil is at the reach of our fingers, ready to be conjured by all, ready to execute our darkest wishes. Maybe evil is an integral part of who we are, of what makes us human. If I let my guard down, if I let my inner drives come to the surface, would they inevitably contain a destructive force? It seems we ascribe evil qualities to some people more frequently than to others. Are those the ones who fail to control their dark inner impulses? If that's so, we're all evil to the core. But that's not what I wanted this day to propose.

I wanted this day to open me up, to bring a certain virginal newness, not the thought of the darkness within. But that's the danger, to look into our nature, that's the danger.

By the time Calixto had concluded that there was nothing to conclude, he was already about a block away from his hotel. He had walked plenty and considered plenty. What was left now was to resume his writing and move beyond doubts and shadows. He then turned a corner and stepped into the street that led straight to his hotel when a rancid smell, a powerful animal emanation, attacked him all of a sudden. When he looked to where the stench was coming from, he saw a man dressed in a striped tunic standing on the sidewalk. He stopped and could not help but to scrutinize the face of this man. And he noticed an angular bone structure stretching a brown leathery skin from one side of the face to the other and a dark hollowness below the eyebrows. Disturbed by the poisonous smell, he gave the man a wide berth and walked straight back to the hotel.

In the quiet of his room, his mind was unquiet. Calixto could not ease his mind into the writing process. The moment he started to write a simple phrase, the image of the strange man standing on the sidewalk besieged him. When he closed his eyes and tried to destroy all images, the strange animal smell stifled his breathing air. He closed all windows and turned the lights off. He concentrated on composing a single sentence. But the presence of the man wearing that striped tunic threatened to imprint itself on the *tabula rasa* of his day. He remained in silence for a while, hoping for time to undue this wicked maneuvering. But instead of fading away, the presence established itself with a sense of inevitability unknown to him until then. Resigning himself to the immediate reality, Calixto gave up all hopes to write a single word and bolted out of his room in search of the man in the striped tunic.

Then came the wind. The early morning breeze that had caressed his encounter with Leda grew into an anomalous force that scattered seagulls and kept flags rigid and horizontal. The old shutters on the old windows flapped and clapped. On the street people bent forward to cut through the wind with their foreheads. Calixto walked towards the place where he thought he had seen and smelt the striped tunic, but he found nobody. He saw a dog barely standing against the wind, holding its body close to the ground, but no trace of the man he had seen earlier. He walked forward to a corner offering a view of the Tejo river. He saw the water snake undulating, ripples crisscrossing its back, boats bobbing. He felt the force of the wind and felt small.

If a force like this one exists, invisible to the eyes of all, how could I replicate its power with words? Words are not seen; they're read or heard. They're symbols, representations. Invisible forces they are, the words. And as I come out on the streets, open to the winds, in search of a smell, of a person perhaps, am I not looking for words instead? Maybe the person I saw, that hard face, that striped tunic, maybe the stench I perceived, are nothing but a compilation of words that impacted me, creating sensations I confused. I can search until dusk for an image or a smell. I can walk until coming across those sensations again. But would I be able to harness those forces and create words or phrases, worthy of the intensity of the winds I now feel?

Calixto took the wind straight. He faced its force. He kept walking around the street where he had encountered the striped tunic. The winds had swept the entire area. The only smell that remained was the ubiquitous staleness of the Tejo. But he kept on walking and looking for that angular bone structure and the dark hollowness below the eyebrows. And just as he was becoming hopeless, he turned a corner and came face-to-face with the striped tunic.

Part II
The Striped Tunic

This nakedness hurts me. The uncertainty hurts me. I hope she will be well…, in the night she will. She will learn to belong to her own self, different from the confused belonging laid upon her. She will need to forget, not the night—she belongs to it. She will need to forget the hurt and those who inflicted it. Nadya, I leave so you can be who you need to be. I leave you so you can exist. And I let go… The waters of the river take me away. I glide, I float, I become the current.

At the train station in Breil-sur-Roya, I cover my body with newspapers and wait at a safe distance away from the sight of regular commuters. People come and go. Those who see me ignore me. Three black men move fast and board a train as soon as the doors open. They do not look back. An old woman stands next to another group of five black men at the end of the terminal. They seem nervous. They do not move much, they simply stay next to the old woman and talk to each other. They laugh, briefly. A few minutes later another train stops at the station. The five men board the train at once, their heads down. The old woman does not say goodbye to them, she just turns around quickly and walks away from the platform. On her way out of the station she stumbles upon me. She stops and looks at me. I look at her.

—When did you get here?

—I've been here for some time.

—When did you cross the border?

—What border?

—Ventimiglia

—The river doesn't know borders.

—One way or the other, you need clothes.

—I need to forget.

—Really…, you need clothes.

The old woman leaves the station in the direction of the parking lot. She quickly returns carrying a pair of pants and a shirt. She offers them to me. I have not worn such clothing in decades. I smile but do not stretch my arms to accept the clothes. She lays them next to me and stands there waiting for me to don them.

—I normally wear a tunic.

—What kind of tunic?

—A striped tunic.

—Are you Moroccan?

—No.

—Where are you from?

—I come from the desert.

—The desert is a big place.

—Yes, it is a big place.

—One of the men from Eritrea left a tunic in my house; I may be able to find it.

—Why would you want to do that?

—Because you said, that's what you normally wear.

—And why would you care about normalcy when you seem to be doing something outside the norm?

—What do you mean?

—Those men are boarding the train.

—What I'm doing is normal. Helping people is normal.

—Where are they going?

—Nice. They're going to Nice.

—And what's normal about that?

—They need to register their abnormal circumstances.

—And then what happens?

—Nobody knows.

—Yes, that's actually normal.

The old woman leaves. I wonder who does she really think I am. I wonder that myself. Who am I, really? She may think I am an immigrant like those she seems to be helping. Not completely inaccurate. But what I escape is not war or financial turmoil. I run away from my past, that past that keeps on dying a little every day. Not the deaths. I do not run away from death. Death is something that needs to happen. Witnessing death does not make any one part of it; it just makes one aware of its existence.

After a while, the old woman returns carrying a tunic over her shoulders. She gets as close to me as any stranger would. This time I do stretch my arms to accept the tunic. The garment is the color of the desert, and that pleases me. It lacks stripes or any other markings. But what touches me more is the aura of sadness weaved into its fabric. A certain desolation, a certain hopelessness makes the tunic heavier than it needs to be. I discard the newspapers covering my body and don the tunic as I have donned many of its kind before. And the moment the fabric engulfs my body, I sense the weight of the old continent over my shoulders. And I accept the imposition, for such is the reality of those who leave behind what they know and what they love. This is a young imposition, the man from Eritrea who left the tunic behind is only at the start of his journey. The continent, Africa, has borne its weight before.

I enter the lobby of the station where common passengers await their train. I wear the tunic with distinction. As I sit on one of the rigid benches, a young woman holding a baby in her arms gets up immediately and sits at another bench far away from me. I do not sense hatred, fear perhaps, but not hatred. The old woman who brought me here sits next to me and whispers in my ear. She tells me to remain quiet and to prepare myself for the arrival of the next train to Nice. She says I should board the train and remain quiet until it arrives at the center of the town. She tells me the police may board the train in the nearby village of Sospel, and if they do, to pretend to be a French citizen. When I ask her what does that mean, she says I should talk about the weather with the officers. The old woman means well, and I thank her for the advice and for the tunic before she walks away from me.

I wait for the train to arrive. And as I am waiting, I wonder why I move away from my past toward an uncertain future. What can the future provide? I leave behind enormous parts of myself. They do not belong to me anymore: the desert is dead, the courtyard in Marrakech was taken by the winds, the professor and the perfumer died together, they failed to find each other, the fat poet joined the moon, the one-armed man was swallowed by his own fears, and Nadya, infinite Nadya, rests secure under my original tunic. Ahead of me lies a large precipice offering space but no answers. I step out of the waiting area and come to the edge of the train tracks. I look south and follow the train tracks with my eyes. The two rails keep a constant distance between themselves. And without touching each other, they stretch their backs in parallel as far as my eyes can see, indifferent about what comes ahead.

When the train to Nice arrives, I board quickly and find a seat next to a window. The car is practically empty, and I enjoy the absence of eyes looking at me, of faces turning away from me. I abandon my body to the movements of the train but hold on to my train of thoughts. I prefer to walk, to forge my way one step at a time. To be taken by the device of fuel and engineering may be a necessity at this time, but one I will dismantle as soon as my needs change. But what are my needs? I know I need to arrive. Where or when I do not know. Many things that could have happened have already happened. So arriving may be an illusion, the sense that something else could happen that has not yet happened. And the likelihood of such a peaceful time or place is questionable. I am moving away, and as a result, I reject my past. Such a stance is reactionary. But are we nothing other than creatures that respond? Would screaming of pain or fighting for freedom make me a beast? Is a four-legged creature different from me?

The train enters a tunnel piercing an inconvenient mountain. For a moment there is darkness. And I know the rail tracks lead the train through this darkness, unquestionably, blindly, expectantly. And if such is the nature of the movements of the train, could I not move ahead with the same certainty? Perhaps I will arrive because the path will take me there. Wherever the "there" may be. If I, then, were to consider my nature as fluid, I would be happy with joining the currents driven by the force of gravity and lunar attraction. I would then arrive at a large body of water, larger than my own body, where my individuality would be softly diluted. As the train comes out of the tunnel, the intense light from the southern sun falls on my tunic, on my face. I feel the heat. And my body absorbs the radiant energy, and I feel an internal and unique sensation of being alive as myself. I turn inside myself and relish in the warmth of my inner rivers. For the moment, I follow those waters.

When the train finally arrives in the center of Nice, I step out and join the crowd looking for an exit. Once out in the open streets, I realize the police did not board the train. Whether I feel lucky about that omission is irrelevant at this point. I have other concerns. At this point, I need to follow a clear line toward the unknown. The unknown contains everything that has yet to happen; that is, everything that exists outside of the desert, Marrakech, or Saorge. I sense the unknown is a vast place, even if I know nothing about it. But I am ready to venture into the unknown, to take what comes ahead.

South from the train station lies the sea. I approach the sea with some trepidation as the vastness proposes abandonment. But the sea seduces me into looking into it. I let the turquoise color overwhelm my senses. I let the colors percolate through me. And inside, I feel an unnatural warmth. The warm air that flooded the courtyard in Marrakech had a drier quality. In the desert, even when I traversed long distances exposed to everything the day and night had to offer, the dry air cut through me like an iron knife without making any promises. What makes this warmth different is its seductive quality. I feel as if something extraordinary is about to happen. I want to believe that magnificence is on its way, but my mind, aware of the idiocy of perceptions, rejects such foolish hopes.

As I look at the sea, I wonder where to go next. I could go back to Marrakech, but the four orange trees would probably be flowerless at this point. I could rejoin the desert and the caravans, but the winds would have probably erased my name. In the mountains of Saorge, people will confuse me with their local murderers. My past does not move ahead like the train tracks, or like the waters of a river. My past is essentially dead. So forging ahead is the only solution, forging ahead with force and conviction. I decide to absorb the sun rays as they lie on me, I decide to gather all possible strength.

I also decide to mark my new tunic, to turn it into the likes of my old one, the one that protects Nadya in her dreams. Recumbent Nadya, of my inevitable silence. In a store selling all sort of tools and irrelevant items, I ask a young attendant for white paint. The attendant asks me what is the white paint for. I tell him I need it to paint white stripes on my tunic. After regarding me for a few seconds, he brings up a can of thick and oily paint. I thank him. I ask him for a thin brush which he provides right away. He then asks to be paid for the paint and the brush. I agree that he should be paid for the goods he provided but that at this very moment I do not have the money. He looks at me and keeping his distance; he tells me to leave the store at once. I would not take from this man anything that belongs to him. I just need to get a little closer to my own nature. He will be compensated, not immediately but at the proper time. I then walk away from the store with paint and brush and head towards the sea. Soon I reach a long promenade that extends majestically from east to west in front of the sea. I descend onto the beaded beach and find a place away from the crowd. Once I settle myself, I pull off my tunic. Naked, I proceed to paint white parallel stripes up and down the tunic as if I was performing an ancient ritual. Nobody seems to care about what I am doing, nobody interferes. The stripes are not perfectly parallel, but they still represent the forward movement, the eternal search for what lies ahead. Once I complete the job, the tunic looks like the one I wore for several years before laying it on top of Nadya. It is not the same tunic, and the stripes are not the same stripes, but the function of the garment remains the same. The exterior world will be separated from my interior world, my body will be covered, and above all, my animal instincts will be contained.

In the mid-afternoon the sun stumbles down the horizon. The rays touch the surface of the sea and bounce towards me. Fractured rays those are. A large silver plate expands in front of me; it boils, it reverberates. I feel the heat. I wonder why the grandness, why the extensiveness. When the realm of our own lives is threatened, the sea seems immense and impassive. Perhaps the sea knows how to exist. It remains calm when it needs to be calm, it becomes upset when harassed by the winds when the moon pulls on it, it yields; but overall, it remains the sea, expansive, deep, engaging. Why are we different? Why do we crest and rise when we could be calm and flat?

With my newly striped tunic, I walk into the belly of the town. I manage to dodge most eyes, most approaches. Step-by-step I move into the core of this town that does not belong to me. I guess, in local terms, I am an immigrant. A strange concept, as I have migrated throughout my entire life without anyone making a point of it. In the desert, everyone is from somewhere else, and nobody cares where that somewhere else is. I sense that in this territory "belonging" is a precious commodity. The more belonging you claim, the more secure you are. I can be wrong in my assessment since I know little about this place. But if Saorge was an example of the rest of the villages in this Gallic country, belonging is preeminent. And facing this difficult reality, I decide to continue my journey south, west, or in any direction that will deliver me to a place of openness.

I understand I am a shadow. And like a shadow, I move back to the train station where being a shadow is almost normal. A train for Barcelona leaves in the next hour. I will board that train. Once in Spain, I could move south and perhaps approach the northern shore of Morocco. But why would I go back to the place I came from? Am I desperate for a sense of belonging even when belonging has nothing to offer? All I have to remember is that my father killed, but I am not my father. I remember the desert made me do things I would now abhor, but I am no longer that person. I should look ahead and forget all those experiences. I should launch into the future and bring my thoughts with me. Even if my thoughts do not provide any solace, I have to bring them with me.

The train for Barcelona is not really the train for Barcelona. It is the train for Marseille. Once I get to Marseille, there will be a train for Barcelona, I assume. Once the train enters the station, I board swiftly and avoid crowded cars or those with children. I find a seat in a corner away from the window. This is a corner for those who want nothing to do with the world. That does not define me. I do want to engage with the world, but the world proposes absurd circumstances I would rather avoid. I lived as a hermit in Marrakech not because I hated humanity, but because the winds that invaded the courtyard were more humane than the humans that roamed that ancient city. I even disrobed myself in Saorge. Yes, I was fortunate to find the kind hand of Nadya, she who preferred to exist in the darkness of the night. But I also found delusional hatred directed at me. So this forsaken corner in this mediocre train belongs to me at this moment. I lean towards the cabin wall, away from the corridor. I cover my head with the hood of my striped tunic, and I hope to be delivered to Marseille later today.

I think I fell asleep. The sunlight comes into the car from a different angle. Perhaps the direction of the train has changed. I look around me and realize that nobody has come to sit next to me. The car is completely empty. I take advantage of the solitude to stretch my legs and arms. I uncover my head and let the sunlight hit me directly on the face. A warmth so universal, so welcoming. And even if this tunic is not my original one, I feel comfortable wearing it. It seems to blend with my skin, with myself. And as I am enjoying my solitude, the door to the car opens up abruptly, and the train conductor steps inside. He takes a good look at me but says nothing. He takes a deep breath and starts coughing. At once he turns around and exits the car. He closes the door behind him with force, vehemently, per-haps with disgust. Maybe the tunic, I do not know.

The train moves at the speed of an easy morning. On the left side, as the train pulls away from Nice, I see the sea, magnanimous, extending far into the horizon, not caring much for the shore left behind. I understand the sea, that feeling of abandonment, that capacity to extend far into the unknown without concerns. For a moment I wish I were the sea. I envy its vastness, its solitude, its beatitude. And I realize the sea has neither meaning nor pity. But the sea I am not, and I am completely aware of that. When I feel defeated, like not measuring up to the sea, the train turns away from the shore and climbs the nearby mountains. When I feel like the sea is my territory, the train makes a turn toward the blue openness and follows the shoreline. I feel the train cares for me. It is a simple machine, the train, but intrinsic in its movements, and in the consequences of those movements, it approaches the likes of a demigod.

When the train finally arrives in Marseille, I move fast onto the platform and search for the next train to Barcelona. I study the time table and discover the train for Barcelona will depart in about two hours. That allows me enough time to rest and collect my thoughts. Barcelona is not where I want to spend my time; it only serves as a corridor leading to the south. And once in the south, I will find my way back to Marrakech. A few seats flank the lobby of the station, and I drop my body in one of them. Once I let my guard down and relax all my muscles, I feel a wind, implacable as winds can be, tunneling through the open train tracks. I join the winds and try to drain my mind of conceptual biases. And without any forewarning, the notes from a violin start an imperfect melody, subsequently followed by a viola, and then a bass. I simply listen to the melody and begin to forget where I am. I let the weight of my body disintegrate, I disconnect from the voices around me and detach from the immediate reality. Then my body feels light, and the striped tunic begins to flutter in the air. The violin plays a beautiful passage, and I follow the notes as they ascend into the sky. But this lovely moment is interrupted by a loud voice announcing the departure of the train to Barcelona. Once back in the realm of those who fail to dream, I sprint for the platform where the train is already waiting. I look again for a corner with no windows and hide my head inside the hood of the tunic. The world remains outside in all its intensity.

*****

Why she enters the car is clear, all the seats are empty except the one I occupy. Why she chooses to sit next to me is perplexing. But that is exactly what she does, with her red hat and red shoes. I simply observe her as she opens her handbag and pulls out a book. She places the book on her lap but refrains from opening it. Instead, she turns her face toward me and gazes into my tired eyes. Her face has a disconcerting intensity. People with those faces have lived improbable lives. We remain facing each other for some time without saying a single word, and I begin to suspect that inside of her, there lives a beast.

She stops looking at me; she opens the book and starts to read out loud. I recognize the text, Odysseus returning to the island of Ithaca, the Sirens, that magical song urging him to plunge into the waves. She projects her voice with conviction. I close my eyes and hear the ancient words against the sound of the train as it glides through the tracks. And for a moment, I feel like I am sailing back to a past that is no longer there. I do not question the words; I just let them take me where they will. She continues to read as the train continues to glide. And the train continues to glide because the horizon is willing to engulf its advance.

—Do you mind if I read out loud?

—For as long as the train keeps on riding.

—Do you think Odysseus should've tied himself to the mast?

108

—He had no choice.

—I don't have a choice either. That's why I read.

—But you choose to read out loud.

—That's not a choice, that's a necessity.

—Are you afraid of silence?

—I'm not afraid of anything.

—I didn't think you were.

—Why the tunic?

—Why the red hat and the red shoes?

—Because I'm not afraid, that's why.

—Are you afraid of the waves?

—No, I don't hear the song of the Sirens.

—How about the song of the beast?

—What beast?

—The one inside.

—There's no beast inside. Everything is outside. Look at my hat, my shoes… I show who I am.

—Do you know who you are?

—Of course, I know.

—But who are you, really?

—Someone who doesn't hide inside of a smelly tunic.

—No, you're clearly not hiding that way.

—Who cares about hiding? Tell me, where are you going?

—I'm going back.

—Back where?

—Back to a past that doesn't exist.

—Then you're going nowhere.

—Perhaps you're right about that. I may be going nowhere which isn't different from everywhere.

—Well, I'm going to Lisbon. That's where they need me.

—Who needs you there?

—Everybody.

—Everybody needs something. The question is what that something is.

—I think I'm something! Not anything, but something! That's why everybody needs me.

When I do not respond to her comment, she turns to her book and continues to read. I fear she may get closer to me or try to touch me. But this may be a projection of my own wishes. However, I do not want to touch her. On the surface of my awareness, I do not want to do that. But maybe below my superficial level of consciousness, I want to rip her apart. I really doubt I harbor such a drive. But for the sole purpose of protective restraint, I sit on my hands, bend my head down, and try to disengage from the experience of having seen her.

She continues to read. And with the turning of pages, the volume of her voice escalates. The gods and the goddesses, the sirens, the sailors, the rocks, the fear of shipwreck. Shipwreck, perhaps shipwreck is what I really fear, not her touch necessarily. I listen to the story and try to remain calm and quiet. But the volume of her voice reaches the point where it overcomes the sound of the train on its tracks. I can no longer hear the march of the train. I can no longer hear where I am going. So I bolt from my seat in one abrupt motion and come to stand in front of her. She then stops reading, crosses her legs, and begins to swivel one of her red shoes. When I manage to hear the motions of the train once more, I sit diagonally across from her. And from this point of view, I realize she is not as young as I had thought, a certain hardness to her chin, the eyes experienced. I have met numerous travelers in my life, in the desert, at the hotel in Marrakech. But I have not met a woman who follows on the tracks of Odysseus with red shoes and a hat. There, perhaps, lies the need. The need we all have for the destruction of our own comfortable expectations.

—Did I offend you with my reading?

—You couldn't have offended me, even if you tried.

—Then why do you sit away from me?

—I'm not sitting away from you; I'm sitting close to myself.

—What's the difference?

—There's no difference. It's all a matter of perspective.

—And from your perspective, what do you see?

—I see you're in need to be needed.

—The only thing I need is to follow Odysseus' journey. Did you already know he would not jump into the waves?

—He protected himself.

—That's what you're doing now.

—I'm not tied to my seat.

—No, you're not. But your striped tunic seems to contain you.

—My striped tunic contains me as much as your red shoes and hat give you away.

—Are we talking about possession?

—No, we're talking about boundaries.

—I don't recognize boundaries.

—I realize that.

—So what would happen if I were to cross over to your side and sit next to you?

—I would probably hear what's buried inside of you.

—And what would that be?

—The beast, perhaps.

We stop talking to each other. She continues to read in silence, and I concentrate on the passage of trees outside the window. I wonder why she wants to go to Lisbon. Because people need her there, she said. But that is unlikely at best, if not delusional. This woman goes out into the world thinking she is needed. This woman wears the color red with intentness. She is not any woman. And as she continues to turn one page after another, in silence, without looking up from the book, the epic story unravels. I wonder what aspects of the story touch her deeply. Is it Penelope? Is it Circe's magic? Or does she identify with Odysseus himself? I can only guess, however, even a woman like her could harbor a beast inside. And that is what I wonder, what is the nature of her beast?

With the passage of the hours the silence between us matures. Not a word has been spoken for a while. In spite of the menacing sense it conveys, I do not stop contemplating her. She is aware that I am looking at her. And I am aware that she is aware. She probably feels needed when I look at her. Even though I do not need her, I do feel compelled to watch as she reads the book. And that is what happens with the passage of the hours, she reads, and I watch.

Outside the train, the world travels fast. Trees, mountains, houses, everything merges into one continuous mass flowing on the other side of the window. I know I do not belong to that world. I do not belong to the world inside the train either. I am just moving, away from my past, but perhaps toward my past. All I know is that I am between one time and another, between one place and another, even if those times and places are unclear to me. And as my mind tries to unravel that which resists unraveling, and as my eyes watch that which behooves watching, I hear the voice of the conductor announcing the arrival of the train at Barcelona Sants.

The woman closes the book and puts it back inside her handbag. She fixes her red hat. Then she turns toward me as if expecting something. I wait for her to speak, but she remains quiet. The train comes to a full stop inside the station, and people begin to exit onto the platform. The conductor announces that this is the last stop and asks for all passengers to exit the train. She continues to watch me as I am watching her. The sound of the crowd begins to die away as people leave the platform to find their connections or to exit the station. We remain alone, in front of each other, inside the empty train.

—The train for Lisbon will depart very shortly.

—You said they need you there.

—They do. But you may need to go there yourself.

—I don't need to go anywhere.

—That's why you need to go there.

—Are you asking me to come with you?

—No, Odysseus, I'm not asking you to come with me. You have your own nymphs to deal with.

*****

The train to Lisbon behaves like a relentless caravan. It stops along the way to take on people, to discard people, to breathe. And those who join the journey expect to be delivered ahead of themselves. By need or by desire, the passengers on the train believe in the future. And in this caravan I come across the same evasive eyes as before, people who turn their faces away from me. An elemental fear boils inside of them. Some of them harbor the beast inside. I am certain of that.

Under the brim of her red hat, her eyes are focused on my presence. Maybe she thinks I am returning to some kind of beginning. Maybe she thinks she needs to protect me. Or maybe she needs to believe that there is some truth in the book she is reading. The many hours ahead will allow for some clarification, or perhaps they will provide none. The train will make a long arch through the north of the peninsula before arriving in Lisbon. And I am pleased to avoid a direct approach, for nothing worthwhile is ever achieved that way.

The only other passenger in the car left a few hours ago when he could not open the window. He must have felt vulnerable. Now there is only her, under the brim of her hat, and myself wrapped in my striped tunic. That external layer, hat or tunic, keeps the outside world from venturing inside, away from the white center inside of us. I wonder what would happen if she were to take her hat off. Would the words of Homer flood the car?

The train heads west at a dismal pace. It tries hard to reach the sinking sun, but it fails. And that opens the door to the dark hours that begin their slow march. The woman turns on the lights in the car. I expect she will adjust her position with regards to the light to continue reading. Instead, she lifts up the brim of the red hat, looks at me, and seems surprised to see me there sitting in front of her. She closes the book and hands it to me.

—Do you mind opening the book anywhere? Just pick a random page.

—What would I do then?

—Just read what's on the page.

—What if I don't like what's written on the page?

—Why wouldn't you like it?

—Because it may talk about returning.

—It may also talk about Penelope.

—I wouldn't like to read that either.

—Why not? It's a beautiful image.

—There's no Penelope for me.

—So you're not returning then. I thought you were.

—I'm not returning because there's nothing anywhere to return to.

The book weighs three thousand years in my hands. Out of fear, I resist the impulse to open it on any page whatsoever. What if the ancient words speak to me? What if the text tells me a truth I prefer to ignore? That is the danger; a book may be bolder than yourself and reveal what you refuse to accept. So I do not move a single finger, paralyzed, I watch the woman as she watches me holding the book. She then points at the book and looks straight at me. Under the brim of her red hat, she holds her gaze for three thousand years. I can bear inordinate pain but not this eternal gaze. So, hesitantly, I open the book and stumble on this passage:

"Come closer, famous Odysseus—Achaea's pride and glory—moor your ship on our coast so you can hear our song! Never has any sailor passed our shores in his black craft until he has heard the honeyed voices pouring from our lips, and once he hears to his heart's content sails on, a wiser man. We know all the pains that the Greeks and Trojans once endured on the spreading plain of Troy when the gods willed it so—all that comes to pass on the fertile earth, we know it all!"

Not wanting to read any further, I close the book and return it to her. She then takes it in her hands as if she were taking me in her hands. And I know that in her hands she can raise a storm. But she then puts the book away and opens her face, her heart, her mind to me.

—I'm afraid of what may happen when I arrive in Lisbon.

—But you told me you were needed there.

—That's the problem; there's an expectation.

—Who expects what from you?

—Everybody expects everything from me.

—Is that a burden?

—Yes, a horrible burden.

—Don't listen to the honeyed voices pouring from their lips.

—I wish I could ignore them, but the song may be coming from inside of me, not from the outside.

—We all have a beast inside.

—Can that beast sing?

—Yes, it can. I've heard its song numerous times.

—Can it be ignored?

—No, you can't ignore it. You have to accept it. You have to tie yourself to the mast; you have to wrap yourself in a tunic, or hide under the brim of your hat.

—And then what happens?

—Nothing happens.

—Nothing?

—No.

The dark hours continue their march. They arrive one after another without any concern for those who resent them. After the conductor announces our arrival in Vigo, the train seems to bear south exposing the moon at the bottom of the sky. It is a moon almost round, almost white. Perhaps a moon that has been maimed. And its incorporeal light enters through the window to shine on us. Under this light, the red hat and shoes of the woman seem less aggressive. Her face looks pale. But her eyes are not softer, still fixed on me, they burn a little. And I wonder what she sees. Perhaps the son of a murderer, perhaps an ancient hero, or perhaps a striped tunic covering a body in flux.

Deeper into the night the Portuguese conductor enters the car. She turns on the lights. At once she walks over to the window and opens it halfway. She inhales a good amount of fresh air and says that it would be better to leave the window open for a while. She turns to the woman whose name I have yet to learn and asks for her ticket. She produces a ticket. The conductor seems content with what she sees. She makes a little hole on the corner of the ticket with the hole puncher chained to her belt. She then approaches me but does not ask for a ticket or anything else. Instead, she turns around and starts talking to the woman in front of me.

—Is he traveling with you?

—He's in the same car.

—Yes, but are you together?

—We're not together, but we're going in the same direction.

—If you're not with him, why do you tolerate the smell?

—What smell?

—It smells like a dead animal in here.

—Oh, no… He's alive. You can verify that.

—Has he spoken to you?

—Yes, he speaks, but he doesn't make any sense.

—I'm moving on. If I were you, I would leave the window open.

When the conductor flees the car, she slams the door behind her. I then get up from my seat to turn the lights off and to close the window again. My life has been invaded by many winds before. I do not need more intrusions. In the calm quiet of the car, under the soft lunar light, I engage with the woman under the red hat.

—What's your name?

—They call me Erendira.

—And who are they?

—The people who need me, they call me Erendira.

—And what do you call yourself?

—I don't need to call myself.

—How do you call yourself in your dreams?

—In my dreams I'm always inside of myself, looking out through my eyes. I don't have to call myself in my dreams.

—So how should I call you?

—You don't need to call me; you're right in front of me.

—You're right, for the moment I don't need to call you.

—What about yourself, what's your name.

—My name is… my name.

—And what's that?

—I don't remember.

—Does anyone ever call you?

—No, nobody needs to call me.

—So how should I address you?

—You can address me according to what you see.

—I see a striped tunic.

—Then, that ought to be my name.

Under the lunar light, Erendira goes back to reading her book. Sometimes she moves her lips as if reading out loud, but I hear no sound. From time to time she looks up from the book. Her face seems transformed then as if the glory or the horror of the story is being played inside her skull. She continues her quiet interaction with the book until she falls asleep. Her chin comes to rest against her sternum, the brim of the red hat covers her entire face. I contemplate the fragmented image of this woman sleeping in front of me. I barely know her. But as my eyes hover above her skin, I sense the vibrations of the ungodly beast. The beast must be taking residence deep inside her body. That explains the ebullient aura engulfing her. The beast is there, crouching, hiding.

Meanwhile, the train continues to glide south, oblivious of the people who travel in its belly. It simply marches at a prescribed rhythm, following the tracks, stopping only when necessary. The train produces its own noise, a machine noise, different from the noise of animals. And nobody is ahead of the train, and nobody follows the train. The train could be a caravan, but it is not. The train could be alive, but instead, it feels dead to me. And I let the train take me wherever it wants to go because I could not change its course. Knowing that it goes south is sufficient for me. Different from Erendira, I am not needed anywhere. The opposite is closer to reality; I feel brutally despised. For the wrong reasons, I suppose… or I expect.

The moon begins to die, not because it wants to die, but because the day needs to be born yet one more time. And as the moon relinquishes its supremacy, I feel its loneliness. The moon parades through the night alone while most of the world turns its face away from it and falls unconscious. I would join the moon in its exodus if I could. But I do not have that option. A yellow light replaces the white lunar light as the train enters the density of a large city. And the new yellow light seems to penetrate deep into Erendira's skin. Inside, the beast is awakened. She begins to toss and turn; she stretches her arms and legs. And from deep inside her entrails she releases the somber howling of the beast. A song dark and powerful, horrifying and alluring. A song she could not hear herself even when it emanates from her own body. Then I realize she is searching. Maybe for love or for revenge, maybe for immortality, or maybe for her own self.

The train slows down its forward motion. Crawling, it continues to penetrate the thickness of the city. The conductor opens the door but does not enter the car. She announces we are arriving in Lisbon. Erendira surfaces from her deep sleep and enters the day. The first thing she does is to turn her face toward the yellow light filtering through the window. She then straightens her body and fixes her hat. Once upright in her seat, she takes a long look at me, as if deciphering who I am and why am I sitting right in front of her. She then talks.

—I see you're real.

—What else could I be?

—A figment from my imagination, maybe a character from a book.

—I could say the same about you.

—Yes, that's the tragedy.

—Would you want to be an illusion?

—No, I'd rather exist, even if that's an imperfect existence.

—Are you imperfect?

—Completely imperfect. Can't you tell?

—All I can tell is that you prefer the color red.

—All I can tell is that you hide behind your tunic.

—Do you think that's an imperfection?

—No, only you would know that.

—I don't know any longer. I really don't.

—Then you must be perfect.

—I couldn't be any more perfect than you are.

—Then we're both perfectly flawed.

—Perhaps, or perhaps not.

The train comes to a complete stop. The light inside the station is not yellow any longer; it has become greenish, somewhat sickly. The crowd descends unto the platform with their luggage, their children. I stay inside the car waiting for people to exit the train. Erendira does as I do; she remains inside the car. And I wonder if she wants to keep me company or if she has no idea where to go. I am not certain where to go myself, other than south. So if she were to depend on me, she would be essentially lost. But she took this train with determination. She wanted to come to Lisbon because this is where people need her. So she should have no reason to waste her time with me. She should step out of this train and head for the place where people are waiting for her.

But Erendira does not leave the car. Instead, she sits up and takes out the book from her handbag. Looking straight at me, as if taunting me, her lips draw a smile before lowering her eyes to start reading from the book. This time she reads out loud, projecting her voice with impetus. She reads for the world to hear, for the world to participate in the experience. Her voice resonates inside the car to the point I start feeling uncomfortable. I stand up and open the window while she continues to project the ancient epic poem out to the world. People on the platform begin to gather outside the open window to hear the poem. And as she continues to project her voice, as she continues to declare the verses written three thousand years ago, more and more people come to hear the story. Her voice ascends and fills the air space inside the car while spilling out onto the platform. Her face becomes as red as her hat and her shoes. And for a moment her voice becomes the story, and she becomes the book. She is perfect. This moment she exists as a perfect representation of the Odyssey.

Then comes the conductor wearing her badge and her crooked hat. She says everyone needs to leave the train. She asks Erendira to lower her voice and then disappears down the corridor. This time she does not slam the door behind her. Erendira closes the book and puts it back inside her handbag. She becomes a silent abstraction, a Homer for those who know no Homer. And I understand why people need her. Not only in Lisbon but anywhere she may decide to go.

*****

The floor of the train station is the color of dried blood, not the color of the reflective eternal sand. People step on the floor, oblivious of the dry blood under their feet. I have stepped on the eternal sand oblivious of its reflective miracle. We all step on something we do not understand. But this is how the world commences. Without a past to return to, the world commences every second. Like when I ran on the river's shallow edge, stepping over dark pebbles, one foot sinking while the other barely surfaced just to sink again in a circular race with no beginning or end. And as I follow the crowd out of the station into the gray outdoors, I lose track of Erendira and her red hat and red shoes. Maybe she was carried away by her own voice. Maybe she followed the song of the sirens. Or worse, maybe the beast devoured her from inside herself. I wonder?

The world outside the station is wide and alien. People move within a gray brume that engulfs every step they take. They briefly re-emerge from the brume only if the sun manages to grace them for a second. Then the heavy brume blankets everything, the street, the park benches, the dogs. I venture toward a wind that rises from the lower streets. I descend unannounced, unseen by most people, under the same brume that covers everything and everybody. I avoid facing the faces that would likely turn away from me. I do not hide, but the brume hides me.

At the end of a descending street, I come to vast open space similar to Jemaa El-Fnaa in Marrakech. But I find no monkeys, no oranges, and no snakes. There are only people interacting with people, or the brume. At the edge of the vast space, a body of water opens up majestically. The gray body of water extends as far as the brume allows me to see. There is no defining line far out on the horizon for there is no defining horizon, only brume. But the body of water ebbs and flows, it rises and plunges like a sea, or like a river that meets a sea. I stand in front of this gray body and consider it as a desert. I stand in front of myself and consider my mind as the sea. And I wonder if all the fluctuations I have experienced in my life have no other purpose but to extend me out into the horizon. If I were to become one with the gray horizon, the events in my life would have had no consequence. And at this moment, just when the world seems to be commencing, I resist to believe that life ahead of me is nothing but gray brume.

The outline of a slender sailing vessel cuts through the brume with brutal elegance. It tacks once, twice, before approaching a dark dock extending out from the quay into the gray body of water. The sails are quickly taken down. A few ropes are thrown to a few hands standing on the dock. The ropes are tightened, and the sailboat is secured. Three people descend from the boat onto the dock. The brume covers their faces and their bodies. I cannot tell if they are content to have arrived or desperate to leave again. They come from beyond the brume, and I wonder what have they seen. Perhaps they can share with me what they know? But perhaps they are only products of the brume, the grayness.

One of the three people that came off the sailboat walks toward me. When the person gets close enough, I manage to see the face. It is a brutal face, perhaps a face that has known the desert. The person starts talking, and only by the pitch of the voice I realize it must be a woman. Even if the deep crevices on her face challenge my gender expectations, the sound of her speech contains a certain tonality not often found in men. She talks at a vertiginous speed, making it difficult for me to understand what she is saying. And the more she talks, the less I understand. I then raise both of my arms and gesture for her to slow down, to stop talking. She stops talking. And the brume is quick to fill the void created by her silence.

I consider this woman and her need to venture onto dry land and start talking to the first stranger that would listen to her. I consider her face and wonder if she has been abused. I consider the impossibility of my presence in front of this gray body of water receiving the nomads of the world. Perhaps this happens because I am a nomad myself, perhaps because nobody else would listen. But I have nothing to offer this woman, not even a past. I hold both of her hands and look with care at her face, at her lips now shut. What I find is a languid desecration, an abominable terrain. I ask her to speak slowly, to tell me what seems to cause her trouble. She then starts talking again at a slower pace.

—Our children have drowned.

—What are you saying?

—Out there, in the middle of nowhere, they threw our two children into the sea.

—Who did that?

—The same people that put us in the boat.

—Where are those people now?

—They also fell in the sea. The brume took them.

The woman starts to sob. She then starts talking again, but her words get trampled by her sobbing. She then runs away from me toward the other two people that came with her in the boat. The three of them have a discussion, they gesture. Then they walk together at a fast pace away from the boat into the grayness. I follow them with my eyes until I no longer see them. What am I supposed to do? I am an immigrant who is facing the world. This woman found me; she shared her distress with me. This woman left me. In the train the woman with the red hat and shoes also found me. And she left me as well. I found Nadya in Saorge. Or perhaps she found me. She did not leave me; I felt I had to leave her. So why do we leave people we need? Why do we need people to leave us? I do not know.

I come to realize that of the thousands of people I have encountered in the desert, within the courtyard of my hotel in Marrakech, in the old village of Saorge, through the many roads and paths I have traversed, across the many years I have existed, the only thing that stays in my mind is the minds of those people. Not all of them, but those that managed to leave an imprint. Our mind is the only valid currency we possess. It is in our power to lend it, to cherish it, to exploit it, to throw it away. Our mind transacts with the rest of the world. And that mind cannot be usurped, cannot be incarcerated, cannot be bled from the outside. Some people wrap their minds inside a body of lies; others build a fortress of insurmountable walls around their minds; others are not aware of what their minds are all about. People could say that I wrap my mind inside a striped tunic. But my mind is not suffocated; it can float through the very fabric of my tunic and come to face the world. Our minds are not open or closed, like our eyes cannot be open or closed, nor our lives can be open or closed. It is all a matter of acceptance, of facing what the world places in front of us, of not running away from the unknown. Because even when we want to shut our eyes, fold inside our lives, or close our minds, we know the unknown is still there.

And I accept this very moment as my personal unknown for there is no other way to interact with the world. Why the woman with the red hat and shoes sat in front of me on the train, I do not know. Why she needed to read aloud out of the Odyssey, I do not know. Whether I will see her again, I do not know that either. And why a stranger revealed to me an improbable tragedy in the gray mist of this plaza, I will probably never know. And what will happen next in this journey to nowhere is a monumental unknown. But in spite of these uncertainties, I will not turn my face away from the mystery, from that which I cannot see, from the unknown that grows in front of me. I celebrate the moment, and I feel free, unbound, true to the very essence of myself, true to my mind.

I embark on the only journey available to me, away from everything that has happened and toward that which is about to take place. And there are numerous old streets in this old town willing to take me there. I chose one street, not because it looks particularly interesting, but because it seems to climb a hill while the other ones remain flat. And as I begin to climb, a sense of foreboding invades my mind. I try to ignore the feeling and continue climbing. But with every step, my apprehension grows. Then a door opens into the sidewalk and out comes a young woman holding the hand of a little girl. The moment the woman sees me approaching, she pulls the child toward her and holds her tightly. I continue climbing. And as I go by them, the woman turns her face away from me while the little girl, curious, looks at me just for an instant and then hides her face in her mother's skirt. If they react in an identical fashion to the unknown, does it mean they are mother and daughter? Is fear of the unknown hereditary? I will never know the answer to that question. So for the moment, I continue climbing. After another block, I stand still on the sidewalk to rest and gather my breath. A man, then walking down the street, stops abruptly and looks at me with interest. I also look at him and notice an expression of yearning on his face. He must be one of those people who search. I would have offered him some mint tea if I were in Marrakech. But this mutual scrutiny does not last too long as this man seems to find in me something disagreeable for he makes a large circle to avoid my proximity and continues to walk in haste. I watch him walk away with a firm step as if he knows exactly where he is going. But if he is certain about his destiny, why would he stop to regard me? He is clearly searching for something.

When I finally reach the top of the street, a gust of wind takes me by surprise. The wind seems to accelerate up the street pushing everything on its way. I hear the old window shutters flapping all around. Above me, a few seagulls balance themselves afraid of falling off the sky. I grab onto my tunic which threatens to fly away. I could let the wind take me where it will. After all, that is what ancient sailors did when they cast their boats off into uncertain waters. The winds took control of their destinies. And the world blossomed. At this moment I consider releasing all of me, letting go of the anchors that barely hold me down, unwrapping this tunic that binds my flesh. I could open the doors to deep desires, the ones that could frighten me. I could flourish from inside my skull.

Resisting the wind, I stand with my feet hip-width apart. With ease, I let my thoughts go where they need to go. I can now taste the sweetness of the unknown. And I am not afraid. I simply exist in the moment. But all of a sudden, a man turns around the corner from where I stand and comes to an abrupt stop right in front of me. I recognize the face of the man I saw earlier. It is a face bursting with fear as if this face was bearing down into the abyss of its own hollowness. And I sustain his gaze, as I sustain the universe.

Part III
Both, The Writer And The Striped Tunic

Calixto

For Calixto, to come across a face that had not bowed to contretemps was momentous. It was the kind of face that existed unhinged. And he found it by chance at the edge of the Iberian peninsula, perhaps at the edge of nothingness. He had encountered loose souls before, some who made an impact on him, but this face spoke a different tongue. If a face could will itself into the world, this one had entered many enclosures; those deep diagonal crevices could only speak of hardship. And for that reason, he looked at the face for a long time. He stayed right in front of this man who exuded a questionable smell, but whose face proposed impossibilities.

Sustaining the man's gaze proved a challenge. Calixto wanted to absorb the full essence of this man's soul. But he could not match the intensity nor the weight of his gaze. He bowed under the pressure. He felt obligated to abandon the eye-to-eye contact and look down to the ground. He felt defeated. But the man in front of him did not seem to notice his discomfort. Instead, he asked him if he was a writer. A bolt from the blue, the question shocked Calixto. Yes, he had been asked that question before, but the fact that this stranger would venture into that inquiry at once molested him. So he answered by saying he was a writer but different from most other writers. When Calixto looked at the man for a response to this statement, he saw the man's facial crevices deepening. Not sure what to make of the reaction, Calixto said he was a writer in search of writing.

There was no verbal answer. And the silence forced Calixto to continue looking directly at this man who was not on the verge of answering anything. Then the wind picked up its strength once more, making the striped tunic flap feverishly, releasing an abundant acrid smell. The man was the tunic, and the tunic was the smell. But Calixto held his ground. He remained standing right in front of the striped tunic while holding his breath until the wind calmed down. Once the world returned to a calmer state, he asked the striped tunic how come he knew he was a writer. The striped tunic then laid on the heaviest gaze Calixto had ever endured, an immaterial force as heavy and palpable as lead. And from underneath the heaviness, Calixto muttered an answer to his own question. He said that perhaps he looked like a writer. The striped tunic, however, said that nothing in his appearance would have led him to believe he was a writer. But that the oblique perplexity he showed when he stopped right in front of him, in spite of the strong winds that were blowing that very moment, could only be displayed by people who wrote about other people. Calixto was not prepared to contest that explanation, so he agreed with a simple nod. Then he added that in his extended walks he often came across a variety of people, some he could not understand, some he could not resist.

After such a confession, Calixto held back his explanatory address. He feared that opening up to a stranger, revealing his anxieties to a man who looked like a beggar, could be a serious mistake. But still, even if he had kept his inner thoughts private, somehow the striped tunic had understood he was a writer. And that level of exposure disturbed him. Not because he was ashamed of being a writer, to the contrary, he would have defended his inclination in front of the world. But the fact that his inner drives were easily identified by this stranger made him feel naked. So he volunteered no other information and resolved to attempt to sustain the striped tunic's gaze.

The two men stood in front of each other without exchanging another word. They regarded each other; they probably developed a theory of the other person's thinking, their motivations, their preconceptions, their biases. They probably concocted a history of each other explaining who they were, where they came from, their city of origin, their parents. They must have dreamed a past that would have detailed a causal chain of events leading them to stand right in front of each other at that point in time. For the striped tunic, the past was probably a dead entity. For Calixto, the past was a conflicting array of forces not yet clear to him. But regardless of the differences in explaining previous events, both of these men were at a crossroad in their own lives.

And that was when the wind became even more vicious. The invisible force swirled and swirled pushing them close to each other. The window shutters clapped noisily as the two men got closer. The dry leaves left altogether, and what remained behind were the solid stones as witnesses. Even the civet smell emanating from the striped tunic was lifted and dissipated by the strong winds. The proximity made Calixto close his fists tightly and close his eyes. He was uncertain as to the danger of such proximity. The striped tunic, on the other hand, had endured desert winds even stronger than that one, so he remained impassive, open to the world in front of him. They both said a few words, but the strong wind took those words and cast them away as dust. Whatever was said did not remain, and for that very reason, the words did not matter.

The striped tunic then started to walk down the street in the direction of the river. Calixto, unsure of what the encounter had meant, wanted to reach for the stranger and explore the reasons for his arrival in this part of the world. But when he took a few steps down the street, the striped tunic turned around and asked him why was he following him. Calixto said he just wanted to know where he was going. The striped tunic said he was just following the roar of the river.

This man is different, unlike so many that have crossed my path. There's a sense of unending to him as if he came from a place far away, yet going towards every place far away from here. Could he be a mere presence? No, he couldn't, he carries too much weight on his shoulders. Maybe he's a future character in one of my books who comes to introduce himself. But that would make him ethereal, and the putrid smell he emanates suggests something blatantly corporeal. He could be a carrier of words. He could be a writer himself. Or maybe he's nothing to the world. I can't tell. He goes to the river because of its roar. I'll follow him. I want to know what the river wants to tell him.

The striped tunic

All the rivers behave alike. Yet they are all born alone at their source and know of no other river unless they experience a confluence, forcing them to interweave their waters with the waters of another river. This happens by chance, not by choice. They all live a life of flowing and roaring until the very end when they meet the river ocean, the one that flows around the circumference of the earth. What if, like all the lesser rivers, I flowed and reached the river ocean? Would I find it to be as vast as the desert? What if the river ocean harbors one or a hundred beasts, all howling and nobody is out in that vastness to hear their song? As I descend to the lower levels of this city, I come across numerous people with languid faces. They may be river people who do not know about the river ocean. Or maybe they think the river ocean flows and flows without ever touching land. But if the land is bounded by the river ocean, the river ocean is also bounded by the land.

Every one of my steps sounds twice as they hit the cobblestones. The first sound is the one under my foot; the second is the sound under the foot of that writer I just met on top of the hill who now follows me at close distance. He seems intent in tracking my movements, for when I turn right onto a side street, he follows me there. I stop walking, and he does the same. And as I continue to walk toward the roar of what seems to be a very large river at the end of an immense empty plaza, he follows my every step. I wonder if this is the same gray body of water I saw under the brutal brume. Perhaps it is. Blatantly, the writer continues to follow me in an open and honest way. I stop abruptly and turn around to look at him. He stops, looks at me for a second, and then turns around to look behind him as if, in turn, he were being followed by somebody else. But there is nobody behind him other than a few frolicking pigeons. The writer knows that I know he is following me, so I turn around and walk all the way to the end of the plaza. Here a magnificent river opens up in front of me. A vast and boisterous body, boiling with life. Its roar is massive, immense, hard to understand. I listen for subtle, simple messages, but the torrent becomes a chorus of unintelligible voices. Then I hear his voice, the writer, who comes to stand next to me.

—Why were you following me?

—The one who followed me all the way down to this river is you.

—Up there, on the hill, you were stalking me.

—What makes you believe I'm interested in you?

—You know I'm a writer.

—Knowledge is powerful. Isn't it?

—What else do you know about me?

—Do you really want to know how powerful I am? Does it matter?

—Nothing really matters only the words we say to each other.

—Then stop asking questions and tell me why do you write what you write.

—I told you I'm a writer in search of writing, isn't that enough?

—It depends.

—On what does it depend?

—On your level of honesty.

—I'm honest; I'm transparent. Can't you see?

—I'm not sure I can see through you.

—What do you see when you look at me?

—Do you really want to know what I see when I look at you? Does it matter?

This writer yearns openly, and he knows it. He allows me to peek into his personal vertigo. People must find him tender, vulnerable. Certainly, people who approach him instigate his doubts. Any mind in a drifting state would want to latch onto him. Those in search of words would be happy to join his crusade for writing. I cannot tell where he is coming from or where he is going. But it seems clear to me he is in the middle of a journey that is confusing to him. Why else would he follow me down to this river, me, a stranger who has offered nothing to him other than a mirror for his own doubts?

At the quay, there are stone steps that descend to the water level. I go down the steps and sit on the last one barely touching the water. I then sink my feet in the cold water and watch them disappear from sight at once. I was cut off from the ground many years ago. I was tossed out of my land. And when my feet feel the freedom of the river-waters, they thirst for a certain belonging. They would grow roots if they could. But that is not at all possible in this middle earth stage in which I find myself. Then I open my tunic and unwrap my body with slow and deliberate gestures. I fold the tunic and lay it neatly on the stone step. I allow my naked body to slide down from the step until the river-waters swallow all of me except for my head that bobs up and down at the rhythm of the wavelets. The cold river-waters surround me, and my muscles feel tense and relaxed at the same time. I immediately remember descending into the

Roya river after leaving Nadya sleeping and dreaming of a longer night. I felt sorry then. Now I feel a certain relief and freedom. Not from her memory, that one will never die, but from the shifting world that surrounds me.

After a few minutes of treading water, I feel a numbness taking hold of my body. With a strong push from both arms and a violent kick against the water, I resurface and come to sit on the moldy stone step. I unfold my tunic and don it at once. Water can refresh the body but not the mind. My past, the dead one, is not soluble. Neither is the uncertainty that lies ahead. Upon the plaza, the writer observes my actions as if trying to unravel a mystery or find a hidden meaning. His expression is softer now. Maybe he finds me just as vulnerable as himself.

The afternoon decides to intervene between this writer's curiosity and my need to avoid people. The afternoon drapes the sky with a certain gray-reddish color that invites isolation and a return to one's own house. I have nowhere to go. I expect the writer will leave and seek solitude at his writing desk. But this is not what he does. Instead, he stands a few meters away from me and continues to watch my every move. He seems to be analyzing and memorizing my gestures. As for what happens inside my mind, he has no way of knowing, although he could be inventing a thread of thoughts appropriate for one of his books. And there he stands, watching, saying nothing, and watching.

My need for a place to sleep becomes more and more intense as the afternoon deepens its colors. I must find a secure place before nightfall. As I look around, I realize this plaza must be the lowest possible part of the city. Multiple streets climb up the surrounding hills promising more secure nooks for the night. Letting chance be my guide, I choose the first inviting street and start walking up at a moderate pace. Behind me, at a safe distance, the writer follows. I turn randomly one way and then the other, exploring numerous streets while still gaining height. The street lamps shed their first yellow light making the city resplendent. And I continue climbing until I come to a landing where the horizon opens up, allowing me to see far into the distance. I cannot tell where the city ends. Neither can I tell where I end?

The writer, who has not missed a single step, comes closer to me and regards the open horizon, trying to figure out what is it I am looking at. There is nothing there but yellow lights and a city that does not end. His expression is not a disappointed one; to the contrary, he seems excited to stand next to me looking out to nowhere.

—Why did you go into the river?

—Why did you follow me up the hill?

—Because, somehow, I need to.

—Then you understand why I went into the river.

—You needed to wash yourself. Was that your problem?

—I don't need to wash myself; I have no stains.

—Then, where are you going now?

—For a while, I thought I was going where the river would take me. I'm not so sure anymore.

—Where do you come from?

—From the same place you come from. A land somewhere.

—Why Lisbon then? What brought you here?

—A woman, Erendira, said she was needed here. She read from an old book about a traveler who could not make it back home.

—Are you trying to go back home?

—I'm going everywhere which is the same thing as going nowhere.

—Sometimes I feel I'm going nowhere.

—Then you must be a wise man.

—For how long will you be in Lisbon?

—What's the essence of time?

—It has none.

—Then, time is not of the essence.

—You must be a writer as well.

—I never wrote a single word in my life.

—That's not possible.

—According to you, it isn't. But that's your prerogative.

—By the way you use your words, I assume you must have read extensively.

—You're confusing words with thoughts.

—What's the difference?

—You know what the difference is, you're a writer.

—I follow your thoughts as you express them by means of your spoken words.

—Yes, but those words are not written anywhere, the wind takes them all away.

—The words remain in my mind; they're written there.

—But you must know that our feeble minds retain very little, and what they retain gets all twisted with time.

—So why don't you write your thoughts down?

—I wouldn't want such an anchor.

—Then write fiction.

—That's what you do, correct?

—I write lies, mainly, not because I want to deceive anyone, far from the truth, but because I think reality is as much a lie as any good fiction.

—You're clearly searching for writing, as you said before, but maybe for something else.

—Aren't you searching as well?

—I already told you I'm not a writer.

—Who are you, really?

—That's a question for another time.

I maintain my pace and continue to walk uphill. The writer stops following me, and I watch as his figure becomes smaller and less significant with the growing distance. I reach a point where I can no longer see him standing on the sidewalk, perhaps because he became increasingly smaller, or perhaps because he just went home. I simply let him disappear from my consciousness. Somehow, I know this is temporary. The writer is searching, and his search will bring him back to me rather soon. How could it be any other way?

Further ahead, in a dimly lit alley, I see a red door. The impulse to traverse it and look for a courtyard with flowering orange trees floods my tired mind. I bring myself to the front of the red door and consider knocking. But before I manage to touch any wood, a woman opens the door and stands in front of me with a resolved expression on her face and a burgundy scarf around her neck. I sense she has been awaiting me for a long, long time.

She steps to the side, and I enter into her house as if I entered into my memories. Nothing on the walls, nothing in the corridor that leads to an inner courtyard where there are no flowering orange trees. I am about to turn around and leave at once when the woman holds onto my arm and leads me to a wooden bench in the corner of the courtyard. She asks me to sit down. I do sit down, and she sits next to me. Then comes a furtive wind, infusing the courtyard with the fragrance of loneliness, that unmistakable smell of bitter almonds. The woman does not react, she ignores the fragrance, maybe because it is utterly familiar to her, or maybe because she does not recognize loneliness. And I wonder why she lets me into her house, why she wants me to sit on this bench. I also wonder why I feel at home in this desolate courtyard.

After a while of nothing but silence, the woman exits the courtyard for a few minutes and returns with a silver tray carrying two cups and a teapot. She sets the tray at the end of the bench and proceeds to serve mint tea. She offers the first cup to me, and I accept it. She then serves herself a generous cup completing a ritual that must be as ancient as tea itself. While sipping from her cup, she looks at me as if trying to recognize a person from a time before this time. What she is trying to identify, I have no knowledge. But the way in which she looks at me reveals a profound loss, a loss hammered by time and disappointment. She then moves her lips as if she is about to ask me a question, but instead she sips more of her tea and continues to survey the territory of my face. I refuse to scrutinize her face for fear of finding traces of those faces I now need to forget. For that reason, I look up to the sky framed by the walls containing the courtyard, I take a deep breath and smell the bitter almonds, and I drink some of the mint tea.

—Your sandals are torn… from walking so long, I suppose.

—They've been torn for a long time.

—What took you so long?

—Time takes a long time.

—I wasn't expecting you, but I was.

—What were you really expecting?

—You, I think. I'm not so sure.

—I came in here because of the red door.

—Yes, the red door is the entrance to this void.

—And what are you missing?

—I miss that which I expect, you perhaps, or maybe someone else.

—Are you missing that which you're expecting, or are you expecting that which you're missing?

—Both, I suppose.

—Expecting will lead you to disappointment. Missing, on the other hand, will lead you to sadness.

—I don't feel sad, but I'm yearning.

—We all yearn, it's human nature.

—Isn't that sad?

—No, that's nature.

I accept another cup of tea from the hands of this woman who must have been awaiting me without knowing I cannot be awaited for because I come from nowhere and toward nowhere I go. But she seems to be experiencing something completely real that does not follow my internal discourse. As the tea flows inside my body, I start to feel more at ease. Then I dare to scrutinize the subtle lines on her face. They tell a story unknown to me. If I were to guess, the story is one of disillusionment. Although that may be the most common story of humankind, I do not recognize her version. If she were to be disillusioned with my absence, she would have been mistaken since I have never departed this place. But if she were to be disillusioned with my arrival, then I clearly do not fulfill the ideal of that which she has been expecting. And that sense of inadequacy makes me feel uneasy.

As time begins to exert its weight, the woman starts to show signs of discomfort. She stops drinking from her teacup, she squirms on the bench, and she loosens the burgundy scarf from around her neck. And there, tattooed on her neck, I see this wonderful salamander that yearns to jump into the world. As lively as the actual reptile, the tattooed creature seems to have been born from fire, and fire it wields with its intense colors and devilish eyes. I cannot help but to abandon myself to the power of this reptile and think of the numerous beasts inside numerous people who never had such a clear representation. I imagine that for this woman, waiting for anyone in the company of such an intense creature would have been miserable, or perhaps illuminating.

The woman notices my interest in the tattoo and removes the scarf completely. She turns her head towards the sky exposing her neck and the fiery creature in its full splendor. Wickedly, she does not look at me as I am looking at the salamander. Instead, she lets me regale myself with the image. After observing her not observing me, I feel a deep urge to reach out with my fingers and touch the salamander. But I recognize I would not be touching the mythical beast but her bare neck instead. So I restrain myself from touching this woman who may have expected my touch. And I realize I may be deepening her disillusionment.

—From what fire did this reptile come from?

—That was a while back.

—Is that what you're now awaiting, that fire?

—I don't know any longer.

—Then why do you show me the salamander?

—I thought you would recognize it.

—I do recognize it. It's a natural beast.

—The salamander or my yearning?

—They may be one and the same. They both sting, don't they?

—Yes, with equal force.

—That's natural.

I recognize this is not my courtyard. I also recognize I may not be the person this woman is waiting for. I might be the embodiment of a concept, but not the person itself. But perhaps that does not matter. If I can satisfy her yearning, would not that be sufficient? Why do we need to personalize everything? In the middle of this courtyard I could represent whomever she wants me to represent. Is that a hazardous proposition? I can also invert the equation and propose for her to represent that which I yearn for. After all, I found her behind a red door in the middle of a courtyard similar to the one in Marrakech. However, I am not exactly looking for her. I am looking for a way back to a place that may not even exist. Perhaps I am looking for the hand of someone who cannot offer me a hand.

On the north side of the courtyard, below the sill of an open window, there is a wooden table on top of which three books rest dormant. There are no other elements, animate or inanimate, in this courtyard. And for that reason, I feel the urge to explore those books and try to find why they happen to be there. The woman, noticing that I am looking towards the table with the books, moves quickly in that direction and grabs the book on top. She opens the book and starts to read out loud. I hear her voice pronouncing words and phrases that make me think of immortality. She then closes that book and takes the second one from the pile. She opens the second book somewhere in the middle and starts to read out loud again. This time she reads in a foreign language, Slavic perhaps. And before she continues reading, I interrupt her.

—Is this your mother tongue?

—If there was ever a mother, this is one.

—What you read sounded sad, or maybe the sound of the words is a sad one.

—Must be the sound of the words because the passage was about beauty.

—Isn't beauty sad?

—How would I know about that?

—You could if you ever lost it.

—I couldn't have lost beauty because I never had any of it.

—You couldn't have any beauty unless you had lost something.

—I'm not going to talk about that.

—Your loss?

—What loss? I haven't lost anything yet. I'm still waiting.

She keeps reading the book to herself in silence. The words must be full of meaning as the salamander on her neck seems to grow and tremble as the blood pulsates under it. The reptile seems to know the story. Then the wind gathers some speed and enters the courtyard, forcing her to hold the pages of the book in place. Bothered, she closes the book at once and removes her hair from her face. She then looks at me knowing very well I did not understand the words, but certain that I felt their inherent sadness.

With hesitation, she picks up the third book and opens it to what seems to be the very beginning. She starts to read slowly, pronouncing words in Spanish with difficulty. She tries hard to intonate and bring life to the text but without much grace. The salamander goes to sleep. She then puts the book back on the bench and throws her hands up to the sky, as if giving up, or as if asking for help.

—You don't know Spanish.

—No, but I should.

—Why should you?

—Because I want to read this book.

—Why?

—Because the author likes bread.

—He must like words too.

—I think he does, but I don't know him that well.

—Is he whom you're waiting for?

—There's no way for me to know that.

—Who's this person, where does he come from, what's his origin, who are his parents?

—All I know is that he's a writer who likes bread.

I take the book in my hands, and it feels surprisingly heavy for its size. Maybe it contains more words than a typical book, or maybe the words are heavier. The title, *No Somos Pero Somos*, implies an existential impossibility. But without reading the book, I would not dare to pass any judgment. I decide not to open the book to avoid an inevitable false impression. However, if this book is important for a woman who receives me in her courtyard without really knowing who I am, then the book must have caused a strong impression on her. An impression perhaps similar to the one I caused on her when I went through the red door. Both the book and I are unknown but somehow expected. Although it would be foolish to infer a connection between arbitrary elements that create a similar imprint, it would be just as foolish to deny an inherent link between them. After all, chance does not exist; it never has.

—Where did you find this book?

—It's for sale at the bookstore.

—Do you expect me to buy this book?

—Not this one. There are more copies at the store where I work.

—Do you work at a bookstore?

—We both do.

—You, and who else?

—My salamander and I. We never leave each other.

—You're interlaced.

—More than that, we know exactly what the other one is thinking.

—Is that a burden?

—No, to the contrary, a relief.

—If I went to the bookstore, would I meet the author of this book?

—Probably not. Is he supposed to be waiting for you?

—There's no way for me to know that.

—I guess there's no way for us to know anything.

—There's no way for me to know that either.

—Well, come to Livraria Mundo. You'll find the book there, maybe the author.

—How do I get there?

—The same way you got here.

Searching, searching. That is how we find ourselves in a place different from the one in which we are. Searching for an answer, for our past, for the object of desire, searching for the expected, for the unexpected, searching for what we lost, for what we will not find, searching for what is next. And in the next few minutes, I will find myself going through the red door and leaving the woman and her salamander in their courtyard, in their void.

Calixto

That morning, in his mind, Calixto had already walked around the world in search of the appropriate words to describe the impression the man in the striped tunic had formed on him. And in spite of its length, that walk had not produced any words whatsoever, but only an uneasy sense of emptiness. He knew he could venture inside his mind one more time or, alternatively, step out into the tangible world to find the words. He chose to step out into the world and walk as he normally did, and perhaps in the midst of such normalcy, the most abnormal words could be found. And those words would not be used in the labor of fiction, or in the artistry of lying, those words needed to touch something more real. He discarded a walk to the river because its fluidity would challenge his sense of reality. That morning he needed to stay close to the ground and feel the immovable solidity of the world beneath his feet.

With impetus and unwavering determination, Calixto ventured out and met a morning that made him feel transparent. His steps found a welcoming ground and no resistance from the green mist enveloping everything. He moved with ease. And possessed with such lightness, he directed his walk towards Livraria Mundo where he hoped to find Lyubochka. She could not provide him with the words he needed, and he knew that, but she could alter his basic expectations and somehow, open a sliver in his mind for unusual words to seep in. And as soon as he gathered some momentum, he thought of bread. He could not enter Livraria Mundo without offering Lyubochka life in the form of bread. He knew bread was important for her. And because he wanted to be fair, he was ready to offer a slice of life in exchange for words.

As he had done in previous days, he walked randomly until finding the aroma of freshly baked bread floating in the air. He followed the trace and reached a small bakery surprisingly empty at that time in the morning. When he stepped inside, a man with a white beard and a white apron asked him what he wanted. He did not translate his thoughts and told the attendant he wanted a slice of life. The attendant asked him what sort of life was he yearning for. Calixto recognized he had spoken what was in his mind without linking his thoughts to the external reality. He corrected his request and asked for any bread soft in its core but with a credible crust. The bearded man said he gave all his breads enough credence, that it was up to Calixto to decide which bread to have. So Calixto pointed at a dome-shaped bread that resembled the world, an appropriate shape to bring to Livraria Mundo. The bearded man seemed to agree with his choice for he displayed an encouraging smile and told Calixto that he would be delighted by the inner and the outer aspects of the bread.

Once back on the sidewalk Calixto realized that, on pursuing the aroma of bread in the air, he had wandered away from the streets known to him. He had no idea in which direction to walk in order to reach Livraia Mundo. He knew that sooner or later he would find the place. But he felt he was carrying the world in his hands and wanted to be certain where to go. So he went back into the bakery and asked the bearded man if he knew how to get to Livraria Mundo. The bearded man heard the question and thought about it for a little while before asking Calixto if he was looking for a specific book. When Calixto said he was not looking for any book in particular, that he was in search of words, the bearded man displayed another encouraging smile. He told him to walk primarily east while ascending as much as possible and then wished him good luck in his writing. This unexpected confirmation of his condition as a writer made Calixto wonder if he had revealed his raw thought process once again. But uncertainty did not comfort him, so he decided to follow the directions given by the bearded man and walked east and towards the sky while carrying the world in his hands.

As he kept ascending, Calixto noticed how his mind felt lighter. Lighter in the sense of the weight imposed by obligations. And the obligations that felt the heaviest were those related to accomplishment, the ones he imposed on himself. Would he be able to source the words he needed? Would he be capable of writing the prose he aspired to write? Surprisingly, those preoccupations became lighter and lighter with every step he took up the steep hills of Lisbon. And just before he became so light to the point of almost floating up in the air, Calixto arrived at the doorsteps of Livraria Mundo. He descended, he took a deep breath, and he entered the bookstore.

He thought of the ocean. He thought of the fire that gave birth to the mythical salamander. He thought of the placid expression Lyubochka had managed to sustain in front of him. And humbled by the overwhelming force of those elements, Calixto walked to the desk where Lyubochka was quietly reading and asked her if she cared for some bread. She regarded him as if he were an old friend, as if he had been standing in front of her for a lifetime. And with the simplest and most unencumbered nod, she accepted his offer. She said that bread was the essence of life and that having some of it at that moment would be just perfect. And without looking at him, she delicately turned her head and went back to her reading. Calixto placed the dome-shaped bread on the desk and proceeded to break a piece of it with his bare hands. He then offered the piece of bread to Lyubochka. She did not stretch her hand to accept the piece of bread. Instead, she turned her head, as delicately as before, opened her mouth, and waited for Calixto to place the piece of bread between her teeth. And in spite of fearing the salamander would lash out at him, Calixto went ahead and placed the piece of bread between her teeth. She chewed on the bread, swallowed it all, and continued with her reading.

Calixto felt as if a massive sun had burst inside of him. And not knowing exactly how to react, he abandoned the bread on top of the desk and went around the store reading book covers at random. He wanted to flee the bookstore as well but contained himself thinking he was on the verge of very important words or perhaps a revelation of sorts. But Calixto knew that neither words nor revelations would come forward without pain. So he took hold of himself and allowed a few minutes to go by while reading from novels in Portuguese. Once his mind felt more at ease, he returned to the desk and dismembered the bread a little. He took a piece and savored it with intensity. He then took another piece and offered it to Lyubochka. She grabbed the bread from his hand, and instead of eating it, she offered it back to Calixto. And just as she had done before, Calixto opened his mouth and waited for her to place the bread between his teeth. And she did just that. He then chewed on the bread and felt another burst inside.

Once they had shared the essence of life, both understood a little more about each other. And a small hint of knowledge could only propel a larger desire for knowing more. This time Calixto remained silent while Lyubochka took the initiative and asked him where was he from originally. He had asked her the same question before, and that placed him in the uncomfortable position of having to answer. But Calixto was not interested in his real origins, just as he was not interested in his real name. So he pondered for a while, walked around the store, opened a few more books, looked outside the door, consulted a large atlas, had another piece of bread, and then walked around the store some more. He then approached Lyubochka who pretended to be immersed in her book when in reality had been observing his erratic behaviors. With certain solemnity, Calixto said he was not sure where he was originally from. Lyubochka ignored his answer because she did not believe what he was saying. So she then asked him to forget about the concept of *origin* and to tell her where was he from. This time Calixto answered at once saying he was literally from nowhere. Lyubochka smiled and caressed the salamander on her neck. She went on talking about her youth and the many places she visited when growing up in Ukraine, many of which felt like nowhere. She said that nowhere was virtually everywhere during those days. And in the same light tone, she asked him if he felt like nowhere was everywhere around him.

So light she is, so seemingly nubile, so close to that nerve. I walk because I need to get somewhere. And once I get somewhere, I keep on walking to get somewhere else. But somewhere does exist, it isn't nowhere. Looking back is more complicated. I certainly come from somewhere, but I cannot find words to describe it well. Like there are no names to name anyone appropriately. In the absence of words, there's no certainty. In the absence of certainty, somewhere could become a ghost of itself, maybe disintegrating into nowhere.

Calixto explained that Lisbon felt like somewhere, that the bread tasted like the life he was living, and that if nowhere was central to his past, it was not a burden for him at that moment. She accepted the explanation and went back to her reading once more. Somehow she sensed it was a delicate question that needed further reflection, and for that reason, she dropped the subject. And what arrived next were minutes of silence during which Lyubochka read from her book, and Calixto continued to evaluate passages from various books he randomly pulled from the shelves of the store. The next arrival came in the form of a man wrapped in a striped tunic who entered the store emanating a questionable aroma.

The striped tunic

A bookstore called "Mundo" must be a crossroad of thoughts. Regardless of any particular language, origin, or destiny, all thoughts are bound to coalesce at some point. Perhaps this bookstore is such a place: an eye, a focus, a crux… Such a place must be devoid of fear. And I have no fear as my hand pushes the door open and I come to face shelves of books and the same woman who received me in her courtyard, now bent over a book, reading in the company of the sleeping salamander. She does not lift her eyes. Unperturbed she remains, maybe immersed in words, or maybe lost in her memories. As my eyes adjust to the dim light inside the store, I come to realize that many of the books are covered with dust. An old world this may be, or perhaps thoughts have ceased to coalesce in this place.

Resisting the urge to approach the young woman, I stand still and wait for her to acknowledge my presence. Sometimes the sands are uncomfortably still ahead of a desert storm. But what begins to move is not her, nor the salamander, but a man that emerges from behind a bookshelf and comes to stand in front of me. At once I recognize the writer that has been following me. This time, however, it was me who came from the world outside and entered this "Mundo." He makes a facial gesture as if wanting to smile, but nothing materializes. He then places a hand on my shoulder. Not a heavy hand, but a hand nonetheless. I have touched very few people in my life, and very few people have touched me. So, with the utmost delicacy, I lift his hand and drop it at the side of his body.

—Have you used that hand to write any words today?

—It's too early to try my hand at writing anything. So far, I'm just reading and tasting life.

—Are you reading your life or tasting your writing?

—That would be hard to answer.

—I know, that's why I ask you.

—I'm tasting bread and reading at random.

—That seems to be a common approach to life. But you don't seem to live a common life.

—How do you reach that conclusion?

—It's not a conclusion; it's an observation.

—How about yourself, what brought you to this bookstore?

—Nothing brought me here. I came on my own.

—But there must be a reason. There's a reason for everything.

—She's the reason, or perhaps the salamander, or both.

Upon hearing my mentioning her, the young woman finally lifts her eyes and looks in the direction where I stand confronting the writer. She does not seem surprised to see me in her bookstore. To the contrary, it appears as if she has been expecting me. She then closes the book and picks up a piece of bread lying on the table. She chews on the bread as if chewing on life. And somehow, I feel the force of diverse worlds coalescing. I turn away from the writer and decide to come close to the young woman as she is enjoying the piece of bread. The expression on her face is utterly placid, even blissful. I consider extending my hand to greet her, but I resist the impulse. I will not touch her. Why touch someone when we have thoughts and words that go beyond the mere physical sensation of pressure over skin? But what if I caressed her face, or taunted the salamander? Both invasive intrusions that would alter the tranquil coalescing of our worlds. So I let my arms hang loose next to my body, and I move forward with my words.

—What do you find in bread?

—It reminds me of my childhood.

—What about your childhood? A dryness, a softness, the breaking of a crust..?

—No, just the feeling of comfort.

—So you feel at ease at this moment.

—I do, but I don't.

—What bothers you?

—I feel as if nothing I expect ever arrives, as if I need to wait forever for everything.

—And what do you expect this very moment?

—Nothing, or everything, or nothing at all.

—But you seem so calm…

—I'm calm because I'm waiting.

—We all expect something. Sometimes, however, we forget what we're expecting.

—I don't know any longer. Maybe I've forgotten who was supposed to arrive.

—How about the salamander? It seems to spit fire with every turn of your head.

—The salamander knows.

—What does it know?

—Nothing, or everything, or nothing at all.

And like a bold desire, the wind bursts into the bookstore and causes havoc with the books, the breadcrumbs, and the moribund dust. The young woman runs towards the entrance and tries to hold the door in place. But the wind does not care and pushes the door with force making its way inside the store. I hold onto my tunic while I watch the turmoil. The writer takes shelter behind a bookshelf and says a few words that fly away. The wind blows, we go nowhere, but the wind blows. And just as suddenly as it made its attack, the wind retreats and vanishes, giving no reason for the assault. There are opened books on the floor, loose pages scattered all over, dust still swirling every-where. The young woman traverses the debris and makes her way back to the desk. She sits down and resumes her reading as if nothing has happened. She bends down to the floor and finds a piece of bread the wind blew away. And with the intensity of a wanting soul, she savors the bread and continues to read in silence.

The writer emerges from behind the bookshelf with a chimeric expression on his face. His hands hold an open book, and he begins to read out loud. The words are in Spanish, a language unknown to me, but the inflection in his voice uncloaks a sense of longing as if something dear has been lost. The writer continues to read, and with every sentence, his voice becomes graver and louder. At the end of what seems like a mournful passage, he pauses to take a deep breath. When he recommences, the young woman joins him and reads out loud an identical passage from the book she has been holding all along. The voices produce identical words with an identical doleful expression al-though their pitches are an octave apart. They continue the duet for a few more lines, creating a gentle sonic wave that probably betrays the solemn meaning behind the words. When they come to the end of the impromptu recital, their faces transfixed, standing among the blown pages and dust, I realize this man and this woman are like tectonic plates that have just collapsed. And just as quietly as when he emerged, the writer disappears again behind the book-shelves leaving me alone in front of the young woman.

—I told you to come to Livraria Mundo, and you did. I said you might find the book and the author, and you did.

—You also told me you don't know Spanish.

—I don't. I just read the words.

—What do you think they mean?

—I don't know what they mean, but I know how they make me feel.

—And how do they make you feel?

—Probably the same way you feel.

—I think you're correct.

—Then I feel that way. That's exactly how I feel.

—Who are you? What's your name? Where do you come from?

—My name is Lyubochka, and I come from the Car-pathian mountains. As for who I am, there's no way for me to know that.

—I think you're correct.

—How about yourself? Who are you? And… what about that tunic?

—Those are very serious questions for which I have no answers at this moment.

—And when do you think you'll have the answers?

—There's no way for me to know that.

—I guess there's no way for us to know anything.

—Again, I think you're correct.

This young woman, Lyubochka, is clearly searching. And it seems she is aware she may not find what she is searching for. The way she approaches an answer just to turn away when she is near. The way she seems happy not to know. She may fear the intensity of the truth, or perhaps she is not afraid of not finding any truth. The salamander seems to ground her, with its fire grabbing her at the neck. This time the beast is not inside her, as it is in most people. Her beast is an exterior one, leaving a wide space inside her to harbor questions instead of fears. She is a woman that can withstand silence. She is a woman unafraid of fear.

If this writer is the author of the strange book I have yet to read, I need to speak to him before he walks away. Yesterday it was he who followed me. Today I am the one going after him. I move among the bookshelves until I come to the end of an alley where the writer is sitting on the floor turning pages of a very large book. As I stand next to him, I discover he is not reading from his own book as I expected, but instead he is browsing a colorful world atlas. The pages display coastal maps of the Iberian Peninsula: all the way from La Coruña to Faro, from Faro to Almería, and from Almería to Girona. So much blue binding the land and the people in the land. I wonder what the writer wants to find at the edge of the sea. He then closes the book and looks up at me. He appears to be distant, in some far away shore, unencumbered, and probably happy. I consider giving him a hand to help him stand up but resist such impulse. He may not want to touch me, just like I do not want to touch him either. From his sitting position, his face at the level of my feet, he takes a long look at my torn sandals. He turns his face away in disagreement. And with impetus, he stands up from the ground and hands me the atlas.

—Can you show me the place where you were born?

—I was born in the desert.

—What desert?

—An open desert where the wind is free to move among people.

—Can you find it in this atlas?

—Probably, but that would not be the real place.

—Why, doesn't it exist on paper?

—Your words exist on paper. Are they real?

—You just heard them.

—I heard them, but I have not read them.

—I didn't read them either.

—So where did the words that you just pronounce come from?

—From my memory.

—A dangerous practice to trust your memory.

—What's the danger?

—That memory relates to the past, and that past may be already dead.

The writer drops the atlas on the floor, altering a thousand dust particles that take to the air making the light filtering through the windows completely visible. He makes his way around the bookshelves to the entrance of the store. There he stops and vacillates between the inside and the outside. But before leaving, he turns back inside the store and approaches the desk where Lyubochka is still reading. He asks her for a piece of bread. Lyubochka looks around for another scattered piece of bread. She finds a piece and brings it directly to the writer's mouth. He does not grab the piece of bread with his teeth. Instead he takes it with his hand and puts it in his pocket. Then he goes to the door, and without hesitating this time, he starts walking down the street. I follow him with my words.

—Where do you think you're going?

—To the edge of the sea.

—And what do you expect to find there?

—The spiral of words.

Calixto

During the night, between one nightmare and another, Calixto stood by the window of the hotel to breathe humid air and to consider the monumental walk from Lisbon to Cádiz. This would be a much longer walk than any he had ever attempted. He could not accurately calculate the number of days he needed to walk, and this molested him. Instead of feeling enthusiastic about the adventure and the massive release of endorphins the extended walk would produce, he felt asphyxiated. But Cádiz had been a point of departure before. The ocean was there and certainly a vantage place from where to consider its vastness. Then he thought about the three women that had recently intersected his life. An abrupt departure from Lisbon would certainly kill any possibility of seeing them again. Although deep inside, he believed those women would follow him anywhere he decided to go. But perhaps what caused a more pronounced sense of asphyxiation was the desire to walk away from the man in the striped tunic. He wanted to feel a strong repulsion against this man; he wanted to create a respectable distance between the two of them. But at the same time, he felt an uneasy curiosity about him and feared that, perhaps, deep inside his mind he yearned for his company. And that last thought kept him up for the rest of the night.

In the morning, Calixto packed all his belongings and told the hotel clerk he had an urgent matter to solve for which he needed to leave immediately. The clerk asked him if there was something wrong with his room. Calixto explained that the only thing wrong with his room was that it made him feel contained. The clerk nodded seemingly understanding but not understanding anything at all. Once on the street, Calixto perceived the unmistakable smell of freshly baked bread. He instantly thought about Lyubochka. And without hesitation, he headed to Livreria Mundo hoping to find her there. Through the door, he went to find her at her desk reading. Not really knowing what to tell her other than he was leaving, he told her precisely that, and nothing else. Lyubochka was not surprised. She then took the copy of *No Somos Pero Somos* that she was reading and asked Calixto to sign it for her. He held the book and took some time searching for a specific passage. Once he found what he was looking for, he asked Lyubochka to repeat after him. He read the passage in Spanish, out loud, and she, in turn, repeated the exact words after him. She then asked what was the meaning of the words. Calixto said he was not sure what the words really meant, and precisely because of that, he was about to go on a very long walk to the ocean, and perhaps beyond the ocean. Lyubochka reminded him that he had already visited Adraga to encounter the mighty ocean. He agreed, but then introduced the idea that all the oceans are not the same ocean and that only the river ocean shared its waters with all other oceans. Calixto then earmarked the page containing the passage and returned the book to Lyubochka. He left through the open door, and that was all he saw of her.

The journey started the moment the smell of fresh bread had dissipated. He walked as if every step would bring him closer to a certain truth, to a diaphanous place. He walked with the conviction that he would find a stream of words unknown to him. Perhaps not unheard words but unheard arrangements of words. And in such spirit, he traversed plazas and streets, bridges and tunnels, always heading south by southeast. He accepted the fact that not all situations along his journey would be agreeable, that the need to eat and sleep could arise at the wrong place. He even reflected on the potential dangers ahead. He could fall ill, or he could be robbed. But what he could not have forecasted was that a certain smell, or a stench perhaps, akin to that of a civet, would linger in the air throughout the entire journey.

On that magnificent March morning, Calixto approached the Tejo and found himself surrounded by thousands of people. It seemed as if half of the city had decided to follow him on his journey. People were enjoying themselves, all at once, walking over the river on a suspension bridge the color of burnt bricks. Halfway over the bridge, he stopped to look back at the city stretching over the hills. A few other people stopped to regard the open horizon, or to dream, perhaps. But the majority of people were intent on reaching the other side of the river, and they flowed like the waters below them.

At a steady rate he walked, and for the most part, nobody noticed or cared about him. This was not his land, not like any other land was his either. Land masses between one coast and another were particularly foreign to him. So he walked from one street corner to the next, along budding meadows, up and down gentle hills, under a sun not too harsh. Ahead of him, recumbent on its back was the promise of words. He wanted to write influenced by the immensity of the ocean, and the ocean circled the land he was walking through, and only at the other end of that trail, once he reached the port of Cádiz, would that ocean be awaiting him. And nothing could stand against his desire, he thought, when suddenly the silhouette of a woman materialized in the distance, growing steadily with every one of his steps. He recognized the shape, but coming across a known person in this part of the world made no sense to him. Even if the increasing proximity revealed a likeness to that of Lulu, Calixto held back his desire to clarify what could have derailed his reasoning and his plans. He simply stopped walking. He stood at the side of the road, still regarding the silhouette attentively, but without looking at her right ankle. The space between the two figures remained static, but not the inner workings of his mind.

There's trouble here. If it's her, then how did she find me? If it isn't her, then how come the resemblance? And if it isn't her and there's no resemblance, then what am I thinking? Three possibilities that promise nothing but complications. Once again the number 3. At the base of this triangle are two people, Lulu, perhaps, or perhaps not, and myself. At the top of the triangle are the three possibilities I just considered. And that makes it an imperfect triangle because it lacks balance. For it to be perfect, it would need to be a triangle of questions only or a triangle of people only. In that case, a third person needs to enter the scheme to bring it to perfection. And that makes me fear the stench floating in the air. Because I know what my senses are telling me. Because I know what my mind wants to resist.

Paralyzed, unable to solve the riddle, Calixto stood at the side of the road and waited for time to pass. He maintained his gaze firm on the silhouette which was as paralyzed as he was. Nobody moved, only time crawled by. The road remained empty; even the sky was void of birds. And Calixto understood he could not wait there forever, that he needed to continue walking if he were to reach Cádiz sometime soon. He closed his eyes hoping to find peace. He found darkness, not peace. But when he opened his eyes again, the silhouette in the distance was no longer there. It had vanished. It did not mean that Lulu, or whomever that person was, had stopped existing. It only meant that he could not see her any longer. Calixto assumed the risk of coming face to face with that unknown entity and started walking once more. He gathered speed, he was at the brink of running, and he kept that forward motion for a while until he found himself short of breath and needed to slow down to a sustainable pace. By then he had left behind the outskirts of the city, and the road began to open up. He did not look back for fear of seeing the silhouette again. Instead, he focused on a cypress that stood tall against the horizon and walked in that direction.

By the time dusk started to suffocate the day, Calixto had walked for several hours. Exhausted, but inebriated by the freedom of walking, he went on to find a place to sleep. The scattered buildings and houses on the country road were not promising. So he had to walk for another hour before coming to a village with a modicum of life. There he went into a small café and sat at a small table. When the waiter asked him what he wanted, he said he wanted a room full of words. Not understanding what he had meant, the waiter asked him again for what he wanted. This time Calixto ordered a glass of Alentejo which the waiter brought at once. He drank that first glass very quickly, hoping to reach a state of placidity and relaxation. But he could not relax much since the few people sitting around him started coughing and seemed truly bothered by something in the air. Some of them stood up and left the café. He could not have offended those people, he thought, he had not said a word to them. The waiter seemed unaware of the problem and seeing the empty glass on Calixto's table, came around and asked if he wanted another round. Calixto agreed. When the waiter returned with the wine, he apologized for the disagreeable smell and said he had opened all the windows to allow the air to circulate better. Calixto drank that glass of wine even faster than the first one. He then called the waiter back to his table, paid the bill, and asked if there was a hotel where he could spend the night. When the waiter asked him if he was bothered by the smell, Calixto explained he was not particularly bothered but that he needed to leave right away. The waiter pointed at a sign down the street and told him there was no other hotel in town but that one. Calixto rushed out of the café and headed straight to the hotel, uncertain if the air had changed around him.

The hotel door was open, but all the lights in the lobby were off. He walked through the lobby, careful not to trip on anything until reaching the concierge table. Then the lights came on, tired lights, bored lights. And a man came down a staircase at the end of the lobby and asked Calixto if he needed a room for the night. He needed a room for the night, but more than anything, he needed to rest his mind. He did not mention anything about his mind to the attendant; he only spoke about needing to rest. The attendant proposed that, if all he needed was rest, he could turn off the lights again and Calixto would be welcome to remain

right there in the lobby and get all the rest he needed. Calixto thanked the attendant for his proposal but requested a
room with a bed and a desk. Upon hearing the word "desk,"
the attendant immediately asked Calixto if he was planning
on writing all night. He was planning on sleeping all night
after walking for several hours, and he made that clear to
the attendant. The attendant then concluded that if he was
planning on sleeping all night, he really did not need a
desk. But that if he insisted on having a desk in the room,
then he must be some kind of writer. Calixto thought about
answering the assertion in a straight and clear way, but he
held back. All he asked was for the room and the bed, and
if by chance there was a desk in the room, he would be
pleased. The attendant seemed content with the answer
and gave a heavy and ancient key to Calixto. He told him to
climb the stairs to the third floor and to try the key on any
of the four doors, that the key would open one of them but
he was not sure which one. He then said that some rooms
had desks and others did not, but that none had bathrooms
inside, the bathroom was at the end of the hallway. And
after saying all of that, the attendant ran up the staircase
ahead of Calixto and turned all the lights off. In the dark,
tired as he was, Calixto waited for a couple of minutes until
he heard the steps of the attendant die away behind the
thump of a closing door. He then grabbed the handrail and
climbed the stairs in full darkness, slowly, until he reached
the landing of the third floor. There he padded the walls
until he identified the first door, he felt for the keyhole and
tried the key. The door did not open. He went on to find another door and tried the key again. The door did not open
either. There were no other doors to be felt on that wall. So

he turned around and pierced the darkness across the landing hoping not to fall down the staircase. His hands then identified a third door. He felt for the keyhole and tried the key. The door opened, and he entered the room. A sliver of moonlight came through a small window barely illuminating the stark room. He confirmed there were a bed and a chair, but no desk. Calixto then dropped his tired body on the bed and fell asleep wondering why the third floor and why the third door.

Through the same small window, a ray of sun broke in the early morning and found Calixto ready to continue his long walk. He wanted to use as many bright hours as possible; he wanted to move far away from the little village and from everything that felt uneasy. He was hoping the attendant would not be waiting for him in the lobby. He had planned to leave the money under the heavy key and depart at once. Down the stairs he went, quietly, like a thief. But as soon as he stepped into the lobby, he heard the voice of the attendant at the top of the staircase asking if he had slept well. He responded that he had slept very well but that he was ready to continue with his travels. The attendant ran down the stairs and came to face Calixto as he was leaving the money and the key on the front desk. The face Calixto saw was that of a desiccated night owl who seemed anxious. He took the key and the money, gave them back to Calixto, and asked him why was he leaving so early. He insisted on Calixto staying longer and promised that if the room had no desk, he would move him to another room. That it was important to make him feel comfortable since not many writers came to the village. Calixto repeated his desire to leave and handed him the key and the money.

And at that point, one of the windows burst open under the force of a strong wind that made everything in the lobby shake a little. The attendant rushed to the window and closed the shutters. But then the front door also opened up with vehemence. And the wind flooding the hotel was not only strong, but it also had a strange quality, as if it had been locked up in a moist cellar for a long time or as if it had been in contact with decaying mushrooms. The attendant shut the door and locked it. He then asked Calixto to excuse him and ran up the stairs disappearing behind a closed door as he had done the previous night. Calixto waited a few minutes in the lobby. He could hear the wind trying to force its way through the windows. The shutters were rattling. When nobody else came down the stairs, he realized the hotel was completely empty. He disliked the sense of that growing loud emptiness. So when the attendant failed to return, Calixto decided to try to open the front door and face the wind.

The striped tunic

This man who writes feels a need to go after his words; this man who travels the earth. But he does so by walking, moving at the natural rhythm of the human body. And I wonder if he finds the words in the very act of walking, or does he really need to be at the edge of the sea to find his words there. Either way, he seems to be in deep communion with nature of which language is only one of its expressions, no different from a mountain or a leaf in a tree. He showed interest in learning about my origins, but he did not speak of where he comes from. He could come from everywhere, just as the words he wields come from everywhere. Perhaps the words require a physical body to harbor them and bring them to existence. In that case, his essence would be a fluid one. But perhaps, he comes from the earth and blossoms from its core. The words are the man; the man is the earth, the earth is the source of many of the words men have uttered. But he seems to be an ocean man.

If he were to see me, he would probably think that I am following him. But I am not following him, neither his words. I am following his need. He is searching for words, he thinks, when in reality he is searching for understanding. And he needs to understand where he and his words come from like I need to understand why my past keeps on dying. In that sense we are not different; we both have a need for understanding. And I wonder what is at the root of such a need, what binds our feet together.

The writer emerges from the hotel in haste. He does not seem to care for what surrounds him. He does not look right or left. Determined, he undertakes his walk at a brisk pace, heading south, aiming at that shore he must have seen in the atlas. As he walks away with the strong wind at his back, the dust kicked up by his feet dissipates quickly. The same wind makes my tunic flap strongly between my legs, and to conceal such noise, I glide ahead towards the south. Along a lonely road, we walk in tandem for a long while. Our proximity is only known to me. He may suspect my presence, or perhaps even expect it. Why else would he have shown me the atlas? Even if he was not aware of his need for my following him, the need was there. And one need leads to another, as one step leads to another and one mind opens another. And so we continue walking, one ahead of the other, on this path to the southern shores. The sun climbs to its highest point and watches our steps, eerily quiet, revealing nothing. And for a few more hours the secrecy of my proximity remains intact.

As the day matures the shadows grow in length. I fear that my dark and stretched shadow will encroach into his reality. So I change my course to project my shadow into the fields and against the lonely houses, away from his body. I must avoid any sudden intrusion into his awareness. I will observe his movements, his turns, his leaps. And through his actions, I will determine his thoughts. And his thoughts will inevitably reveal what sort of beast resides inside him. As he is not different from every other man, he harbors his own, personal beast inside. And this I will do stealthily, in the quiet of a near distance.

When the night arrives, it finds us both exhausted. We have walked a great stretch of this world in one day. Yet, the writer seems intent in walking some more under the stars. He must be looking for shelter, or perhaps for the morning light. Ahead he continues until reaching a small enclave of houses where a few lights still shine through the windows. He turns a few corners until coming to a desolate plaza where he drops his body on an empty bench. He lies on his back, exposed to the night and the universe beyond this night. And as I watch him from afar, I wonder what he thinks of himself. Does he consider himself as a distinct entity or as an indissoluble part of the universe? Perhaps the words he uses link him to the great vastness. Or perhaps he is seeking a deeper connection by means of his words. But the connection already exists. His inner beast and the great vastness of the universe are made of the same material. They cannot be separated from each other. Just like my tunic and my body; they are one and the same. And even my past, in its dying form, belongs to the future of the universe.

I can hear his breath, soft now, placid, unencumbered by dreams or nightmares. And I observe as his body melts over the bench, his arms dripping on either side. He seems relieved to have walked so long. Even if the shore is far away, he seems to find peace in his total abandonment under the open sky. This leads me to believe the writer belongs everywhere, that he is a native of every land in the world. But he may not be aware of this reality, a reality I cannot impose on him. And for that reason, I need to maintain a safe distance. I shall not influence his search, his process of discovery. He needs to walk alone.

The wind dies down and the night reaches a beautiful stillness. I come to rest between bushes with fragrant white flowers that remind me of my past life among orange trees. I pull the hood of my tunic over my head and close my eyes. My mind travels back and forth in time. There is no use in holding onto my thoughts now. I let them fly away.

Calixto

Calixto had expected a long walk, but he had not anticipated the loneliness. One day of walking followed another day of walking where interactions with passersby were minimal. He began to think about the surprising encounters he had experienced in Lisbon. How the smell of freshly baked bread led him to women, he was now missing. He felt the need for company. And without realizing it, he started to suspect the image of Lulu he had seen on the road was an illusion. He then wondered if all the encounters he had in Lisbon were illusions as well. This was a disturbing thought he dismissed at once. He knew how to play in the fields of the words, in the diaphanous fictional space. But his mind always stayed in touch with reality. And there was nothing more real than traversing the world on foot.

The act of walking, especially when the walks were extensive, created a sense of vacuum in Calixto. A short walk did not have the power to produce a void, but the long ones were more challenging. After laying his head on a pillow, or a bench, tired from thousands of steps he had taken during the day, he felt as if a rush of air flooded into his inner vacuum. In the last couple of days, the air seemed laced with a pungent smell he could not clearly identify. Maybe the farmers were spreading manure on the fields; maybe the land was getting old. But this strange experience did not dissuade him from pursuing his goal. He simply accepted the flow of air in its natural form and continued to walk.

Walking south promised a future ocean. The ocean promised a vastness from where words would naturally emerge. Words would interlace with each other to produce provocative prose. He would then shape the prose and construct his next novel. His next novel would deliver him to a realm beyond that of *No Somos Pero Somos*. And in that realm, perhaps, he would feel completely integrated with every writer that had existed in time. After all, every one of the words in that novel would have been used in a similar context and with a similar intention by some writer in the past. He realized that literature could not be re-invented, that the highest goal was to commune with every writer of every time, past, present, and future. He wanted to feel free to literally play in the fields of the words.

So Calixto walked and walked some more. The hours behind him and the hours ahead coalesced to form a river of time. And in that river he navigated south, passing villages and fields, people and their miseries until he reached a massive wall of stone. The majestic wall had a square bastion in its center from which a purple flag flew with pride. Behind the wall was the old city of Cádiz. And behind the old city was the ocean. The Phoenicians, the Greeks, the Romans, and the Moors had arrived before him. They had all settled in Cádiz at different times to look out to the ocean, to marvel at the possibilities.

Calixto made his way through the narrow streets, convinced he was at the end of his journey. From this point forward he planned to move ahead by means of his words, not his feet. Cádiz offered him a promontory in front of the ocean from where to extract the words he needed. In spite of the excitement of reaching his destination, he acted with the utmost care not to reveal his identity as a writer. This time he wanted to remain anonymous, like a shadow. So when he walked in front of a bakery where the twisted *manoletes* were on display, he resisted the urge to enter and continued to walk ahead. He did not want to meet anyone by chance or by destiny. He preferred to bear the loneliness than to risk his progress.

After walking around the maze of white buildings and asking numerous people, Calixto finally found a small *pensión* willing to rent him a room for an undetermined amount of time. The room was the size of a matchbox, and the wallpaper was peeling off. But it had a small window that opened out over the ocean, and below the window was a desk with a chair. That meant everything to him. He rested his feet, but his mind carried on seduced by the warm air and the potential for words. Once his mind settled, and he felt the weight of having arrived, he got on his feet and took to the streets again. The purpose was not to walk in circles around the city but to buy a bottle of *Jerez* to celebrate his arrival. And not even a block from his room, Calixto found a simple bodega where he bought the fortified wine. Back in his room, he rested his feet again while enjoying the first glass of *Jerez*.

This is the soul of the earth. This wine is the blood of all the cultures that have dominated this land for the last three thousand years. I partake with them in the experience of living. They must have felt like I do now, content to have my feet grounded while looking out to the vast ocean in front. We are the same people, with the same dreams, the same fears, and the same need to express that which we harbor inside. By painting on the walls, by hammering the stone, by singing, by stringing words together. We need to usher out the creative lava inside of us. The wine helps, there's no doubt. The wine does to the mind what the blood does to the body; it keeps it alive. But there's a limit, I know. Too much wine and the mind loses its way. Too much blood and we need to apply leeches. But at this moment I celebrate my place in the fluid continuum. I raise a glass to honor those who came before me.

By the time Calixto felt restored, the moon had made its appearance and was reflecting a simple and clear light. Outside the window, the ocean had turned into a black undulating surface marked by silver streaks. He felt like touching the ocean with his hands. So he left the room once again in search of the shore. The streets were lively at that time. People paraded with a sense of abandon as if all that had to happen had already happened and there was nothing else to worry about. There was a vibrating energy connecting everyone on the street as if all the bodies were evenly tuned. People were talking to each other with vivid enthusiasm. He tried to understand the themes of the multiple conversations to no avail. The voices grew in volume and rose to an unintelligible level. As he went through a narrow alley, he came across a young woman leaning against a wall and singing alone. He managed to get her attention and asked her why were people so happy. The young woman said she did not understand his question and continued singing. Again he tried to ask her what was causing the euphoria. The young woman said that nothing was causing the merriment other than the clarity of the moon. Calixto looked up at the moon and found it clear indeed. But he had seen many moons before, some as clear as that one, and that had not made people so euphoric. Then the young woman told him to go to the beach where the moon was at its clearest.

The voices of the celebrants became fainter and fainter as Calixto made his way to the shore. In front of him, the ocean grew, it's black body vast and heaving. He took off his worn-out shoes and left them on the dry sand. Gradually, he walked into the lapping surf until he was knee-deep in the water. He felt grounded and fluid at the same time. That was the provenance he was searching for, extensive, connecting all the people in all the continents. He then bent and tried to grasp a moon ray reflected on the surface of the water. His hand grabbed only water. He then listened for the words of past writers, but only the sound of the surf reached his ears. He looked up to the moon again and found it extremely clear. And he felt a certain bliss.

Then came a gust of wind from the ocean and a salty spray bathed his face. The force of the wind began to mount. Right in front of him, the moon rays revealed a herd of white horses galloping over the ocean's back. They jumped from one wave crest to the next, their white manes bursting in the air. The wind emboldened, lifted the sand on the shore giving off a smell of rotten algae. The stench was as rancid as the wind was strong. Calixto admired the violence of the elements, but as the surf began to ram against his chest, he decided to retreat to dry sand. When he turned his back on the ocean, he was shocked to see the man in the striped tunic standing at the edge of the surf. The white stripes on the tunic and the silver streaks on the ocean were one and the same.

The striped tunic

At the edge of the ocean, the writer looks for his edge. The surf traces an eternally undulating line of convergence. In front of him I stand, not as the ocean, but as an undulating counter-reality. His feet are dry and wet and dry, in response to the ocean. My eyes are open and closed and open, in response to the reflected moon rays. Outside of this moment, there are other moments, but this is the one that concerns us both. So I try to forget my past, and I hope he will try to ignore his future. And the river-wind tries to bring us together with its fluid force.

—What do you feel when you immerse your feet in the ocean?

—Maybe the same you felt when you immersed yourself in the river.

—But those are different waters.

—And why does the river seek the ocean?

—Because it has no other choice.

—And why do you insist on following me?

—Because we both respond to water.

The writer seems perplexed to stand between the ocean and me. He could dive into the heaving waters and swim to any land he wishes. He could also ignore me and return to the safety of dry land and the squalid room he rented. But he came here for a reason that will not resonate with any of those options. He came here to search for words. But in spite of the massive weight, the search imposes on him, a sense of peace surrounds him now. Under this clear moon, he seems lighter, almost weightless. Maybe he has found something, as unlikely as that may be. Or maybe he is getting used to my presence.

This writer must have a past. Even if he behaves as if the world is only about the moment, he must have a land he belongs to. Even if my own past is in a continuously disintegrating matter, that does not mean the writer shares the same conundrum. Why else would he flock to the very edge of this land, one of the most ancient shores? From where he now stands, voyagers have taken off to the unknown. And he may be seeking for such an opportunity. But to leave it all behind requires a land to treasure as your past. His impetus, his desire to venture, demands rooting. And in such elemental reality, we differ. He who seems to launch ahead extricated, me who lives an extricated life who wants a sense of rooting.

In total solitude, a stone bench rests a few meters behind me. This bench endures the salty air and the weight of humanity on its back. It does not move; it remains planted in front of the ocean. I come to sit on the bench and continue to observe the writer as he walks into the surf and out of the surf as if probing the limits of water. Far in the horizon, the moon illuminates a faint line where the ocean seems to bend away and cascade over to the west. The writer leaves the water behind and comes to sit next to me on the stone bench. For a few minutes, neither of us utters a word.

—What draws you to the ocean?

—Everything started there… you, me, the whole world. If it is the source of life, it must be the source of words.

—Why don't you enter the ocean?

—With my body?

—No, with your mind.

—That's not possible

—You're a writer, aren't you?

—I would suffocate.

—Are you afraid of death?

—Only sometimes. How about yourself?

—I'm not afraid of death, but of the loneliness afterward. In the meanwhile, parts of me are dying every day.

—What parts are you referring to?

—My past. It keeps on dying.

The wind starts shifting from south to southwest. Then an aberrant wave crests over and spreads itself all over the sand almost reaching the bench where we are sitting. The submissiveness of this sand reminds me of the dunes in the desert, those sand dunes that were continuously reshaped by the burning winds. The desert, the desert… The desert of my past exists in its proper shape as landscape. And the current condition of my memories is the desert of my past. Then another impetuous wave reaches close to our feet, and as it retreats, it scars the sand forming ridges that will be cured by the next wave. Do we only remember the visible scars? What happens when brutal insults leave no marks? I am certain the scars of the mind are real, and we remember them for as long as our memories are alive.

—But I do remember aspects of my past. Perhaps the way you remember a book you wrote a while ago.

—I forget what I write in my books almost as soon as I finish them. I must read them again to know what really happened.

—Aren't your books part of your life?

—As much as your past is part of your life.

—Then your books are dying as well.

—Perhaps, but I can always find a copy and read them again.

—As you see, I cannot relive my life, so the death of my past is imminent.

—Why don't you write about your past?

—I don't court vanity.

The writer responds in a short phrase, but the wind blows the words away before they reach my ears. I regard him and notice the steadiness of his expression. I sense he is determined, but I am not so sure what he is really determined to do. We remain in silence witnessing the battle of wind and ocean. Fluid forces, immense forces that shape each other. We hear the loud words of those fluid forces without knowing what they say to each other. An ancient discourse, I suppose. Then the writer gets up from the bench and starts to walk towards the village. A clear night this is.

Once the figure of the writer begins to vanish, I leave the stone bench behind and follow him under the clear moon. He mixes with the crowd in the streets but does not seem to interact with anyone. He is part of the tumultuous body of people celebrating in the middle of the night, but at the same time, he is completely separate. And that can only happen when the beast inside is growling. That which he searches, those words he yearns, are already brewing inside of him. The creative process must have unfolded under the bright light of his unconscious. And the beast can speak in words the bearer cannot listen hear. But at some point in the night, the beast will howl. A deep and uncloaking howling that will be. I want to listen to that howling.

Through the maze of streets, he walks. The moon whitewashes the white buildings, making them radiate in ancient glory. He accelerates his pace as if wanting to burn his path. Perhaps the urge to write has taken hold of him. I keep up with his pace at a distance, never to close. He then comes to a small plaza completely open to the night sky.

There he stops abruptly and regards the clear moon above. I remain in the periphery of the plaza hiding among the moon shadows. The writer talks to the moon. He enters in a one-way conversation with the whiteness. What he says I cannot hear. He could be asking the moon to lighten his path. He could be asking the moon about a distant shore. But the moon does not respond; it has no answers. I wonder if he knows that all the answers are already inside of him.

After this brief interlude, the writer continues his walk until reaching the white building where he will spend this and many nights to come. He is absorbed by the front door. And a couple of minutes later, a light shines through a window that opens in the direction of the ocean. The writer has entered the realm of the words. I am certain he feels safe inside that room. No wind to fight, no disappointing moon, nobody following him. There he can allow for the words to emerge as they wish. I do not expect he will turn that light off the entire night. How could he?

Then time becomes fluid. For a long while, I hear nothing, only the lapping of the waves of time. But I know the writer is writing. Inside his mind, the words are coming together into sentences and paragraphs. I cannot imagine the themes; I cannot imagine the images he sees. I do not yet know what his fears are. But inside his mind, everything is converging, turning past and present into the same unit of time, mixing the real with the unreal; facing the elemental anxiety of not knowing what will happen next, distilling life drop by drop. And all the sudden, in the middle of the bright and quiet night, I hear a doleful cry as if uttered by a haunted animal. A possessed sound that comes from deep inside the writer's room. There is the beast; there is the howling.

Calixto

Calixto wrote uninterrupted for the entire night. He observed the changing angle of the moonlight as it filtered through the window. Transported by the moonlight, he received the words he was waiting for. And he received them in abundance. At first, the words were loose, unattached to each other, seemingly unrelated. But as they stirred inside his mind, they started to make sense. He realized the words somehow referred directly or indirectly to the man in the striped tunic. The associations were at first unintelligible. But he then came across the words "noisome," and "rancid" and knew at once what the signified was.

The verbs carried unusual force, and the nouns created elliptical associations unfamiliar to him. He knew he had started to write irreverent prose, precisely what he was yearning for. He carried on with abandon, not holding anything back. At one point in the writing, he tried to hammer out a description of the man in the striped tunic. The description attempted to combine the various impressions he had had since they came face-to-face in Lisbon. But as he put the words together, he became nauseous and had to vomit to release himself. Calixto worried he would fail to write an accurate impression of the man. He thought he had not seen enough of him, and even the little he had seen was revolting. He then considered exploring the fears the man elicited in him. At first, he resisted the impulse. However, the pull was magnanimous. And the more he wrote, the more painful it became. But undeterred he continued, knowing that his text was existing outside of pleasure, that bliss could only come with new disturbances.

The morning light arrived and found Calixto drained. Outside the window, the ocean was showing off its blues. The air was calm then. He realized he had written the whole night. The text glowed in front of him, but he would not dare to read a single sentence. He turned away from the text and continue to regard the ocean. He thought of the many sailors that had taken off from those shores. Many of them had no idea where they were going. Many of them never returned. And of those who returned, many of them left again. He understood them; he had walked thousands of miles and was familiar with the urgency of departure. But Calixto had always arrived somewhere at the end of his walks. Every one of his walks had a clear destination. He had yet to fall off the edge of the earth. But the writing he had done during the night was a different departure. It did not feel like walking as usual, but like swimming in obscure waters, unable to breathe sometimes, unanchored, without a north star. He had never vanished in the process of writing. And so afraid he was of where this new writing would take him, that Calixto allowed himself to fall asleep. And he drifted.

The sound of thunder woke him up in the early afternoon. When Calixto looked out the window, a gray curtain of rain was blocking the ocean view. All surfaces inside the room were moist, the wallpaper, his skin. The steamy wetness bothered him. He considered leaving the room to explore the old city and find some bread, but the rain seemed to gather strength. He then took off all his clothes and sat naked at the desk below the window. There he confronted again the writing he had produced the previous night. It seemed like an enormous creature with a mind of its own.

He would have read one or two passages in regular circumstances, but he did not dare to take a look. Trapped by the rain, the humidity, and the unruly writing disgusted him. So Calixto got dressed and bolted out the door into the rainy afternoon.

Under the rain, he walked led by his sense of smell. After a few turns right and left he arrived at the bakery he had seen the day before. Inside the bakery, the air was warm and dry. Then came the overwhelming wave of the smell of life. Calixto rejoiced in the surge and asked for a traditional *manolete*. He relished on a piece at once, and his mind traveled to Lisbon and the seemingly random encounters he had with women who liked bread. Without any success, he tried to decipher the meaning of those encounters. Perhaps those were irrelevant moments in his irrelevant life. But the intensity of the experiences and the oddity of the various women could not be easily attributed to chance alone. For a moment he hoped that one of those women would walk into the bakery and ask him for a piece of bread. But the rain kept most people indoors, and nobody else seemed to want bread at that time.

The rain continued to fall on Calixto and his bread as he made his way back to the room. He knew the ocean was testing him. It brought a mass of humid air from the north and dumped it at the shore and over the old town. He needed to be patient. The air would dry out, and the ocean would show its face again. And as he waited for the rain to stop, his expectations began to change in nature. He would venture out once more, not to look for bread or *Jerez*, but to go to that stone bench on the shore where the man in the striped tunic would certainly be waiting for him. He wanted to come across that leathery face. A turbulence of words had been unleashed the previous night, and he wanted more. That man had spoken about a dying past, a past on its way to extinction. He knew that could be a horrible past, but it had the potential to source a million words. And if the intensity of that past matched the intensity of the face, he would have words to write for a century.

The striped tunic

The writer will come to the ocean tonight. He knows no other option. There is that beast inside prompting him to come to the edge. And that beast needs my consciousness. He has walked long distances and written books before. But this is where he will find his absolute beginning. The future ahead of him is a blank page. And he cannot get away from his commitment to fill that page. And as soon as that page is complete, another blank page emerges. The absolute beginning is as vast as the ocean and as deep as the writer's soul.

On this stone bench, wrapped in my tunic, I await his arrival. I withstand the obtuse gazes of people who walk by. Nobody comes close to me. Even the surf folds back into itself before reaching my feet. The seagulls, however, take their risks. Screaming for food they come around and peck my tunic. They want my flesh. I gesture with my arm as if tossing food out to the shore. They recognize the gesture and move away from me hoping to get some food. They find nothing.

The night begins to settle and the rain withers away. If the moon reaches the same clarity as it did last night, I will look deeper into the writer's mind. There I will find the words he wrote last night, the words that taunted the beast. He must have reached deep inside his fears; he must have come across an image of himself. Of this, I am certain because the beast becomes aroused only when we regard our raw selves. He is unaware of what happened. He could not have witnessed his unconscious looking at his unconscious, which is why we can never come to know ourselves completely. And perhaps, this is why, on this bench, I wait for his arrival.

In front of me, the river ocean undulates and begins to reflect the moonlight. I step up and approach the surf. In the act of dipping my hands in the river ocean, I am touching the entire world. As the river ocean circles the world it touches every shore. And those shores extend beyond the coastline, reaching further inland towards the towns and villages where people live and die. Even if the world is unaware of my touch, I am aware of the connection between us. And by touching the waters, I am touching people. This kind of touch I prefer for it is pure and unaffected. As I look out into the horizon, I see nothing but the openness, so vast that it is hard to fathom. And like the blank page the writer confronts, this openness is an absolute beginning. And if I can touch the world by touching the river ocean's waters, so can the writer touch the world by writing on the undulating blank page. He touches the entire world even if the world is unaware of his touch.

When I turn around and regard the stone bench, I find the writer already sitting there. He has arrived. As I had predicted, the writer attends the instinctive meeting of our minds. He comes empty-handed, without paper or pen. If he is to discharge his function as a writer, he will be doing so from memory in the solitude of his room. I know that is what happened last night. The beast howled when he tried to write his visions of the day. I imagine the same miracle will take place tonight. Or perhaps the same horror.

—What draws you to the ocean tonight?

—The same reasons that drew me here last night. I'm in search of words.

—And what would happen if the words you find end up hurting you?

—There's always that danger, an intrinsic danger to writing.

—So you don't mind getting hurt, it seems.

—Not exactly. I don't mind writing, even if it hurts me.

—Then you must have been badly hurt before.

—Yes, while writing the book you heard me reading in Lisbon. There are many painful moments related to that book.

—And what's the pain about?

—I'm not completely sure of what causes the pain. That's why I need to continue writing.

—To extend the pain?

—No, to understand it better.

I come to sit next to the writer. Under our combined weight the stone bench remains impassive in front of the ocean. The writer, however, wrings his hands and shuffles his feet back and forth on the sand. Perhaps my proximity is disagreeable to him, or perhaps the pain has started to boil inside of him. I settle my gaze on the confines of the horizon and study the faint line between the two darks. The sky and the ocean reflect each other's darkness, but they are distinct from each other. And my predicament and that of the writer reflect each other, but we are also distinct.

—What makes you believe understanding could somehow reduce the pain?

—I imagine that by understanding I would be assigning a past to the pain. Then I could distance myself from it.

—Be careful with the past. I can die without you wanting.

—Have you already lost portions of it?

—Some, but not all. I still remember the desert and the caravans. The extensive movement under the extensive reach of the sun. Our lives didn't matter much; it seemed. That's when I learned about death. It was imposed on me.

—Who died there?

—That's impossible to know with certitude. Death existed in the desert; I know that. And death certainly continued its work once I left the sand and sought shelter inside four walls. But the deaths that coincided with my time in the desert were momentous. And most came not by the force of nature, but by the force of murderous hands. A man against another man. But the most painful was the death of my imperfect father, a murderer himself. When he stepped out of jail, the old man looked older, broken, his vacuous eyes hovering in the dead center of round shadows. One day I went to offer him mint tea and noticed his eyes to be heavier as if the weight of the shadows had become unbearable. I called his name, but he did not answer. I tried to raise him, but the body had no lift, no upward movement, it simply sank. And when the rigor stiffened my father's body, and the air stopped moving through his lungs, I understood the finality of my imperfect father.

—So you achieved some understanding.

—More precisely, I came to realize the impermanence of all things.

—Is that what led you to seek shelter?

—With no one to call my kin, I wandered through the desert, unable to rest my head. Eventually, I went through the city walls of Marrakech. There I stumbled upon a decrepit building with multiple rooms around a barren courtyard where a fountain grew green algae. There I remained in self-confinement, officiating the lives of voyagers like yourself. And there a man and a woman, both in a desperate search for each other, had the unfortunate chance to actually find themselves.

—What happened to them?

—Death happened to them. She wasn't aware of the beast she harbored inside and he wasn't at peace with himself. I saw through them. I saw their fears, their hopes, and their desperate search for something they could not see. I saw the vacuity that comes from not being whole. She created a perfume the likes of which I've never encountered again in my life. He played the music of his childhood, a bridge to a time he apparently never understood. And they coalesced under the open sky of my courtyard where four flowering orange trees witnessed their demise.

—By looking at your face, I can tell your past must be as immense as the ocean.

—But I don't know the future of my past. What I just recounted may not exist tomorrow, either by lapse of memory, vulgar shame, or simple indifference. It is completely possible for events to vanish, leaving no trace. Or perhaps, the traces are those deep ridges you can see on my face. But I only have one face, not dignified enough to honor the lives of so many that have disappeared.

The writer regards my face with consummate attention. Under the bright moonlight, he seems to carve through every deep ridge unearthing a lifetime of turbulence. I remain steady and allow him to explore at will. He seems as brave as he is curious. And he carries on with his exploration until the wind becomes enraged and makes my tunic flap vio-

lently. He jumps back and steps away from me. As if afflict-
ed by a nauseating sensation he turns towards the ocean
and begins to breathe hard. He takes all the air the ocean
can offer. He must be sourcing words, I think. He must be
integrating the words that emanate from the ocean, from
my body. And still seemingly revolted, the writer runs towards the village. The moonlight follows him, and so does
the wind, and my consciousness as well.

Calixto

Inside Calixto's mind, a tumultuous insurrection erupt-
ed. He needed to reach his room and unleash a legion
of words on the blank page. He needed the catharsis to
happen at once. But the narrow streets boiled with people
celebrating life. The dense crowd forced him to slow down
his pace. He went from running to walking, to merely getting by. He took one side street after another to find yet
more people talking, drinking, and smoking. The intense
celebration had taken hold of everyone's time and the night
stood immobile.

Pushing his way through, Calixto came upon an open
plaza completely occupied by the uproarious crowd. He
tried to cross through the middle but made very little head-
way. He then started to make his way around the periphery
of the plaza when he came across the shadow of a woman
resembling Lulu who stood alone at the portal of an old
building. He stopped and regarded the image with suspi-
cion. The moonlight revealed a profile identical to the one
he had seen before. He could not understand the tenacity of
this woman who insisted on following his steps from Nice
to Lisbon and then to Cádiz. And he wondered if she had
been following him for even a much longer time without
his awareness. She could have been a presence all along,
perhaps since he started writing. The tumultuous insurrection inside Calixto's mind soared.

Step by step Calixto approached the silhouette of Lulu.
He took care to keep his face covered as he advanced at
a slow pace. Then a young woman bumped into him and
asked for a cigarette. Calixto made the gesture as if giving

her a cigarette but there was nothing inside his hand. He then pretended to toast with a group of three men but had no beer bottle in his hand. He established a conversation with two women that were not listening to him. He became a silhouette of himself in the middle of the ebullient crowd. And unnoticed like a chameleon, Calixto reached the portal where Lulu was standing and looking at the bright moon. He came as close to her as he could without touching her. So close, he could hear her placid breathing. Then he tapped Lulu's shoulder, and that made her turn around to face him. He saw the face of a woman he had never seen before, bright under the moonlight, almost radiant.

She's not who I think she is. The image is not the person. But why do I keep on seeing the image? Why does the image follow me? Or, could it be that I'm the one following the image? No, that's not possible. She must be walking next to me, side by side. Maybe we always have an image that walks next to us. But what's the purpose? She doesn't talk to me; she doesn't reveal anything. She only makes me think that I'm seeing Lulu. The illusion sustains the illusion.

When Calixto finally made it to his room, he opened the window and looked out to the ocean. He felt connected to the striped tunic by way of the moonlight and the flowing air. And without wasting any more time, he started to write. The words flowed like a torrent. He found it difficult to channel the voluminous amount of images, feelings, and ideas. He began to tell a story based on what the striped tunic had told him on the stone bench. But the writing took a turn of its own. Time lost its essence. The past became the present, and the present became the past. The dead people the striped tunic spoke about emerged among the living. The desert became the ocean, and the ocean became the desert. And when he wrote the word "sun," the word "moon" appeared instead. For a moment Calixto thought he had lost control of the writing. The tighter he wanted the process to be, the looser it became. He felt as if he was looking down a precipice. But he knew that discomfort was at the heart of sublime, disinterested text. So he held back his reign and allowed the writing to write itself.

In a writing trance, he remained for a time unknown. The wind came through the window at will, and the moonlight continued to shed its light. And nothing in his writing changed until the moment Calixto started to describe the smell that emanated from the striped tunic. Then he became conscious of the writing process and had to stop to seriously consider the words. The first association he came across was that of the civet. The cat-like animal whose fecal and nauseating essence could become a radiant, velvety, and floral scent. He then thought of shame and imagined what the smell of shame would be like. He considered decay, death, and rot. He remembered the wounded beggars of large cities and their sordid presence. But none of the words or associations sufficed to accurately describe the olfactory experience of standing next to the striped tunic. He came to an impasse. So he gave up writing for the night.

The room felt small and confining, the air insufficient. Wanting to expand his lungs, Calixto stepped to the window. While looking outside, he realized that it was almost dawn, that the hours had passed without him noticing. Only a few people traversed the street below, most of them alone, a few dragging their dogs. The celebrating crowd from the previous night had vanished completely. At that time the morning had yet to propose anything. Accepting the void, Calixto went back to what he had written during the night. He was surprised by the number of words. Not only were they numerous but also marvelously interlaced. But even after reading through numerous pages, he could not decipher the nature of the story. In front of him was a text which felt intimately his own, and at the same time, alien. He confirmed the central character of the story continued to be the very man whose essence he had no words to describe.

The time of innocence had come to an end for Calixto. That morning he understood that his writing was not ultimately his. He felt connected to the universe by a flow of words outside of himself. He was not a conduit; he knew that he still decided on the order of words and the acuity of adjectives, but he was not a writer independent from the writing of every other writer who ever wrote before him. Writing, then, was not different from life. Our lives originate from the lives of those who have lived before us and share intimately with the lives of those around us. And he took comfort in that thought.

He would have loved to go walking in the misty morning, but the weight of the long night of writing felt like lead. The writing was safe, he thought. The mysteries in the writing were intact. The small window would not allow for any words to escape. So, confident that the integrity of the miracle would be preserved, Calixto let himself go deep. The wind continued to enter the room at will. The ocean held the world as usual. And when his mind was resting, life existed as life. His lack of awareness did not leave an imprint.

Later in the day the sunlight filtered through the window and bit Calixto's leg. He felt the warm bite and woke up not knowing where he was. For a moment he existed as if floating in a vacuum, unattached to any time or country. But the instant he saw the open window, he recognized the place, himself, and the impending writing. The first impetus was to read again what he had written the night before. But he resisted the impulse and put the writing away. What was written was already written. What needed to be written next was the only thing that mattered. And he foresaw that his night walk would take him to the shore, to the stone bench in front of the ocean where the striped tunic would very likely be reciting his life. But this certainty created a sense of doubt. Why would the striped tunic be waiting for him unless he had an essential need to tell the story of his life? He had insisted on the impending death of his past. Was he trying to save that past by recounting it? He, himself, had a past that had never been recounted. So why become concerned with the past of someone else? Yes, he was a writer, but writers have no obligation to tell any particular story.

The hours flowed completely unconcerned about Calixto's rumination. He served himself his first glass of *Jerez* to prepare for the expected. Ahead of him was the ocean with its waves and peculiarities. The stone bench could not move from where it lay. The striped tunic, with his unconceivable smell, would be waiting for him. He then served himself a second glass of *Jerez* to prepare for the unknown. Where would the writing take him that night?

The striped tunic

If I were to sail beyond the curve of the horizon, I would certainly arrive at the port of Tangier. But if I could reach all the way to Essaouira, as the crow flies, then Marrakech would only be a short distance away. I wonder what version of myself I would find there. My hermetic self could no longer exist inside the courtyard. That self would have died by now. Or perhaps, that self has been kept alive by the four flowering orange trees. And if I were to find my old self, would I recognize it? From within my current self, the world seems wide and distant. But this is the only world I have.

In the late morning hours, people come to the shore to bathe in the water or to bathe in their reciprocal gazes. There is merriment. However, nobody comes close to me. I sit on this bench alone, in contemplation of the human exchange developing in front of me. I recognize the archetypal gestures that have always existed: the quest for closeness, the desire to dominate, the need to seduce, brutal rejections. But these are the lives of others; they do not pertain to my world. And no matter how many hours I regard the human interaction, nothing occurs that will change the universe.

By the time dusk invades the shore, very few people can be seen roaming around. The sky becomes preeminent now; it appears grander than the ocean. It signals that other shores exist awaiting their turn to be touched by the night. And all we have to do is close our eyes and wait for the night to deliver us there. But the night has the tendency to make us confront the past. And this is what I fear most at this hour, the crushing advance of my memories, that vast legion of dead soldiers. When I try to lift them up, to entice their fighting spirit, I find that dead memories have no war left in them.

I imagine the shores of Essaouira and wonder if my memories would breathe a different life there. Would I need to withstand the same type of assault as I do now? Would the dead soldiers continue to confront me? Why would it be any different? At any shore, no matter where, the waters of the river ocean are all the same. But perhaps, the closer link to the desert that once bound my feet would liven up my past. A treacherous thought that is.

I see the writer far down the shore walking in my direction. His steps seem light, unencumbered. He must have dislodged a certain gravity from inside himself. Maybe he is learning how to tame the beast. Or maybe he is just oblivious. I cannot tell yet. But, clearly, he does not vacillate, he walks straight towards me. I knew he would return tonight. How could he not? And like an empty galleon, he docks at this stone bench looking for his bounty. He seems tired but eager at the same time. His face reveals a profound expectation. Yes, he may be expecting something from me, but most likely he hopes to embody his own expectations as a writer. I wonder what those expectations are, how real they are, how attainable?

He begins by saying nothing. And I accompany his discourse by remaining silent as well. A time of innocence this is. Then gradually, I sense the emergence of a dialogue inside my mind. The telling of a story, or perhaps a confession. I am not sure. If the ebullient words are mine, then it must be a confession for I have no desire for storytelling. And since I have nothing to confess but my past, this must be a resurgence of events I may have forgotten. Some people may refer to that internal dialogue as memories. But memories are nothing but our own confessions. We confess to ourselves in order to find peace with our past actions. And as the words become louder, I let them out of my mouth.

—Have you paid attention to the roar of the river?

—Right now I only hear the ocean in front of us.

—This is not an ocean, the river ocean this is.

—Then I hear the river.

—Why don't you write what it tells you?

—I would, but I cannot understand what it says.

—But you understand what I say to you this moment.

—Yes, I do.

—Then you know exactly what the river ocean is saying.

The writer regards me with keen attention. He wants to listen to my internal confession; he wants to get the words he needs. I do not resist. I let the words arrange themselves in the necessary order to elicit a past that escapes me. And the images flood my mind, they swell, and I flourish. I do not fear the past. How could I? The past was ordered; it occurred as if perfectly orchestrated. The present, however, shows itself with no consideration for order or sense. It wants to happen on its own terms. So I let it take the shape it wishes.

—Through the river, I reached a village where I had no ties by birth or ancestry. There, a woman brought me food and wine in the middle of the night. Others weren't so kind.

—Where's that woman now?

—She's probably looking for the longest night.

—Do you miss her?

—Do I miss her…

—Yes, do you feel for her?

—I feel for her, deeply. And we spent a night together that could have been the longest. But then came the horror. A horror that only humans can bring upon each other.

—Can you speak of it?

—No, I won't speak of it. It pains me to this moment.

—So where do you store those painful memories?

—My body is the only thing I own, and this tunic to protect it. I'm completely alone with no room to hold memories. The memories go through me; I cannot hold on to them.

—So what happens to your past?

—My past is nothing other than a big hole. My present: this bench, the ocean.

—And if you were to think of your past as your present, if what you thought today were a reflection of your past, what would you then remember?

—I remember I touched a man, something I had not done in years, and in consequence I killed him. He could only make use of one arm, the other one was already dead, but with that single arm, he wielded paranoiac hate.

—What did this man do?

—This one-armed man committed a crime against humanity. He murdered a poet, a gentle spirit who fed words to his mules and sourced words from the moon. And he shot him in response to his anomalous hatred. I had no choice, I had to touch him.

—Do you always kill everyone you touch?

—I don't touch people.

The writer shifts his body away from me on the bench. He creates enough distance between the two of us to prevent an accidental touch. This does not bother me as I am used to people keeping their distance from me. But in spite of his space considerations, he seems interested in what my confession may bear. He waits for me to continue talking. Somehow, he expects me to divulge the story of my past. But I have no desire to share my consciousness. If there is a story within me, if my past could be construed logically and with appropriate sentiment, then all there is to be had is a lie. Nothing can be held within a body that cannot hold anything.

—Why did you follow me all the way to Cádiz?

—I didn't follow you.

—So how do you explain your presence here?

—What makes you believe that I'm present here? I'm the bench and the ocean. My presence isn't mine. You, on the other hand, wanted to come to Cádiz with a clear purpose.

—But that doesn't mean you didn't follow me here.

—You walked here on your own. You have a need, and you pursued it.

—And you followed me.

—I have a need, and I pursued it as well.

—Do you mean to say that we have the same need?

—Do you find that possibility troubling?

—I just need to write my book. That's what I'm after.

—So we happen to coincide in time but not in purpose.

The writer gets up from the bench and walks towards the surf. The moon still shines, but it has lost some of its luster. While last night it seemed eternal, tonight the moon appears slightly maimed. But the writer does not care for the moon. If he had known the fat poet from Saorge, he would understand the moon has the power to extricate words from inside any of us. At this moment he only cares for the tongue of the ocean that comes to lick his feet. I get the impression he is a sensualist. But as I observe him, I realize he does not conform with getting his feet wet; he steps on the back of those ripples where the moonlight shines the brightest. He may still be a sensualist, but that inclination may serve the very purpose he espouses.

—Would you tell me your name?

—My name…

—Yes, how do people call you?

—I haven't been called by anyone in a very long time. And if I ever had a name, it now belongs to my dead past.

—So, how could I refer to you?

—What's in front of you this very moment is the only thing you can refer to.

—In front of me, there's a striped tunic.

—Then that's all there is to refer to.

—But there's also the ocean.

—Yes, but we're not the same.

—Then there's only the striped tunic.

—There's nothing else.

—What about what's inside of you, your thoughts, your desires?

—Just listen to what the river ocean is saying.

The writer then starts to kick the water, sending droplets up in the air. He does so with intensity as if he wants to walk on the surface of the ocean. The moonlight penetrates the water particles and makes diamonds out of them. And the frenzy unravels in front of me. The light, the water, the writer, the words, my past. The writer then sheds all his clothes and immerses himself in the river ocean. The more he thrashes in the water, the more diamonds fly up in the moonlit night. And then he starts to swim away from the shore, deep into the arms of the river ocean. He swims like a dolphin, into the water and out of the water, but always following an elongated moon ray that extends far into the edge of the night. And then the wind starts to gather speed. It blows from the land towards the ocean as if wanting to embark on a long journey. And the waves begin to crest, and the moonlight jumps from one wave to the next, creating jagged angles and broken paths far into the edge of the night. I look out in search of the writer but cannot see his body any longer. He cannot help but satisfy his need. He is going deep into the source. He wants to listen to what the river ocean is saying.

Calixto

He floated on his back, Calixto, and his recumbent body moved up and down under the moonlight. The waves behaved like benevolent angels at the service of the ocean. They could have swallowed him, but they spared him instead. In reality, the ocean did not mind that Calixto had pierced its undulant body. So the ocean allowed him to continue floating on its vast surface. Finally, the waves and the wind returned Calixto's body to the shore far away from where he had started his swim.

He crawled until he reached dry sand, and there he stood, overwhelmed by the numerous words he had gathered from the body of the ocean. He was alone, naked, but ecstatic with his bounty. All he needed was to return to his room, if he could find it, and immerse himself in the writing process. So he took to the streets of the old city hoping to find his way. He went for the darker streets, avoiding the clear moonlight that would have revealed his nakedness. He waited in the shadows for people to pass by him, he dodged all lamp posts. But the white buildings reflected the moonlight so perfectly that Calixto was inevitably bathed in the nightglow. Trying to become a shadow turned out to be impossible.

Calixto then decided to shed all fears and expose his naked self. So he took to the streets running at full speed. He went by people who were surprised and amused at the spectacle. But nobody tried to stop him; he ran unopposed. The speed he kept made him miss a few turns and to confuse one street with another. But he eventually managed to reach his room without a major accident. Once inside the room, he opened the window and looked out to the ocean. He had communed with that immense and fluid body. He had extracted a wealth of words from it. And he trembled. The sweat dripping from his entire body got mixed with the blood trickling from the cuts on the soles of his feet.

I feel whole in this nakedness. I extend beyond myself. People wouldn't want to see me this way, but this isn't about people. This is about the bodies that hold the words. I wonder if that man ever sheds his striped tunic. The stories and words he harbors inside must be immense. And he only insinuates a few details from inside that shell. He says his past is dead, but maybe his past is only covered. Maybe he needs to swim in the body of the ocean as well. If his body were to merge with that of the ocean, the fusion of words could be exceptional. Or maybe he just needs to get rid of that tunic and let his past come alive. There's so little I know about him. The inverse is true; he seems to know me, he seems to see through me. He must know how I feel in this nakedness.

After opening the gates of his unconscious, Calixto started to write abundantly. He did not even bother to get dressed. He silenced the internal critic and allowed the prose to gallop unbridled. For Calixto, every day contained a moment when he thought he would touch immortality, what followed next was the stuff of novels. He considered the relationship between an artist and reality to be an oblique one, and indeed, in his judgment, there was no good art that was not consciously oblique. If he wanted to respect the reality of the world, he knew that he could only approach that reality by indirect means. And the path he was following that morning was an obliquely unconscious one.

The hours and the words accumulated. He had no desire for food but did not skip on a glass of *Jerez* every so often. In an effort to transcend traditional narrative, Calixto needed to wield words under the constraints of the novel's tremendous weight. Consequently, he needed to discard many rules to bring forth this vision. On that account, he was creating an anti-democratic experience that promised to leave out the middle-class, or middle-reader, the populous group which had generated the traditional novel. He explored the inner world of the striped tunic, experimented with non-linear formats, employed multiple points of view, embraced philosophical constructs, used lyrical language, and made clear and not-so-clear allusions while not explaining everything in an expository way. He was writing outside of the traditional mold, but he was not the first, nor would he be the last one. His challenge was how to manage that difficult and complex task, how to pull off the high wire act without crashing down to the floor.

I would like to know what's the ultimate purpose of writing novels. What's the real value of reality in fiction? Should the novel be clear and open to all? Who are the readers? And in a more existential vein, does it matter to the universe whether I write a novel or take a piss in the ocean? When the path becomes an ocean, and the waters burn, when a step is nothing but a dream, when leaping forward grows flowers on my skin… I then know I'm a writer. So I plunge, deeply.

And ahead he continued until the dawning of the hours. And he saw no respite during the long day. Finally, consumed by hunger and exhaustion, Calixto wanted to rest. But the desire to feed his mind with words and to be in the presence of the striped tunic was stronger. So he barely dressed and took to the streets. He did not care if the streets were crowded or empty if the wind was calm or beastly. He walked towards the stone bench in search of the essential elements that sustained his writing. And the closer he got to the ocean, the faster his heart rate became. And his steps gathered force, and the walking became a furious run towards the shore. Fast, fast, faster…

Calixto reached a point on the shore from where the bench could be spotted in the distance. He then gathered all his strength and went for a final sprint. But as he got closer, he stopped his frantic race at once. The shape of the person sitting on the bench was not that of the striped tunic. It was the familiar silhouette of Lulu. He did not know if his eyes were telling him the truth. After a full day of writing fiction, the world had become somewhat unreal. So Calixto closed his eyes and waited some time, hoping the image would dissipate. If he were to open his eyes and the image of Lulu was still there, there was a chance it was really her. Difficult to explain, but possible. If upon opening his eyes the image would have vanished, then he needed to explore his expectations or go even deeper into his unconscious. Regardless of the outcome, he knew a piece of reality had become dislodged.

When he opened his eyes again, Calixto saw with clarity the loose shape of the striped tunic sitting on the bench and looking out to the blurred line between the ocean and the darkening sky. After calming down his breathing, he launched towards the bench at a normal walking pace. His concern with the vision of Lulu would not be unraveled then. At that moment, what mattered to him was the striped tunic and the ocean. And both were there waiting for him.

He came around the bench and sat next to the striped tunic. He tried to find the spot on the horizon where the striped tunic was focusing. But what Calixto saw was a vast body of water blending with the vast body of the night sky. He wanted the striped tunic to continue talking about his past. But all he got was silence. The striped tunic remained motionless and did not say a word. And even when a light breeze came from the ocean, it carried only white noise, not a single word. There he was, in front of the essential elements, deriving nothing from them. He feared death, or perhaps oblivion. Calixto then wondered if the striped tunic was indeed sitting next to him. So he closed his eyes again and waited.

I cannot decipher him. I might be able to write an entire book about him and never know who he really is. Perhaps he may reveal himself to me if I reveal myself to him. But I get the sense he already knows me. He knew I was coming to this bench tonight. He prepared himself to receive me. In silence, that is, but here he is. Or, is he not? Is he only a product of my fiction, a mere embodiment of words I have written down? And if so, what difference would that make? I need to open my eyes now. I will open my eyes.

The striped tunic

—How far are you willing to go?
—I have come very far already.
—You have only come as far as it is comfortable. Are you willing to venture further?
—In search for words?
—You think you're looking for words, don't you?
—Yes, I've been looking for words, and I've found them here.
—This is only the portal. Look at the river ocean in front of you. It extends far into the horizon; it touches every shore. Land is the secure ground of home; the ocean is like life, the outside, the unknown. There are words out there, and much more.
—But I cannot take it all.
—You don't have to take the river ocean; the river ocean will take you.

The writer looks spent. I am not surprised when the beast howls there is no rest to be had. He went into the body of the river ocean last night, and I believe he found some words. Not only has he found them, but he must have written them down. And tonight he comes back to this bench because he believes in continuity. What yesterday procured, today will likely procure it again. A comfortable thought that is. But if he wants to identify his real need, he would have to take to the ocean and go beyond this night. I will take to the ocean myself. But I will do so to rejoin my past, to start over again.

This night is the preamble; he does not know this night is the last of its kind. Ahead is the next phase of both of our journeys. Different journeys those are but intimately inter-laced. If he were to join me, which he will because the need is already there, he will source the words he yearns for. He will also find himself in a different place from this place. And as I think these thoughts, I regard his long and tired face and wonder if he has the strength to carry on.

—I told you about the longest night.

—The one that brought horror and pain?

—Yes, but on the longest night, there's room for more than horror.

—What else is there?

—There's everything: hope, joy, mystery, marvel, pain for sure, perhaps eternity.

—Has anyone ever experienced a night as long as that?

—Probably not, but we all want to live through it.

—Is that what you're after?

—Perhaps, but I'm after my past at the moment. The longest night may be there for me eventually.

—And what do we make of this night?

—This will be a long one indeed, but not the longest.

—It already feels heavy for me. I can barely stay awake.

—Again I ask you, how far are you willing to go?

The writer does not respond to my question. He turns away from me and deposits his fatigued gaze on the hori-zon. I imagine he wants to float on the water, or perhaps he would like to sink into it. He can see the horizon just as well as I can. For him, it represents the rest of his life, his life in words, his life as a wanderer. For me, the hori-zon is nothing other than the natural extension of the river ocean. And by means of the horizon, by reaching out to its confines, I will arrive at the same point from where I started. And in so doing, I may commence a past anew. We will both take to the ocean tomorrow. And if the winds are fair and fill our sails, we will dock in Essaouira after two nights. From there we can make our way to Marrakech, by foot if he prefers. But I have yet to find out how far he is willing to go.

—The ocean is the path. Behind us is the land you already know. Burnt land that swallows your past as well as mine. You came to the shore because you recognized the limit. You're standing at the limit right now, and it doesn't move. You went beyond the limit last night when you entered the waters. And you found your words, and you saw some of yourself in the words. Stop weaving dreams in your mind. Because the only thing we have, of men, are their words.

—But how can I follow that path? By drowning like the rest of them?

—Come and join me, we'll sail together. Now go back to your room and rest if you can. Collect the material things you need and come to this bench by high noon.

—Where are going?

—Look far into the horizon. That's where we're going.

In the early morning, I reach the port where a bearded man prepares his boat for sailing. I observe him for a while. It appears no passengers wait to board the boat. A younger man, his only crew I suppose, helps him get the boat ready. I approach them when they sit down to have coffee in the cockpit. After talking for a while, I explain we are two people who want to reach Essaouira. The captain's plan is to sail as far as Casablanca where he has some business to manage. He agrees to continue further south if we work as crew. In that case, he would dismiss the young man. He would not have to pay him, but he would not pay us either. He clearly wants to keep his money. And I clearly understand that he is a smuggler. He seems suspicious of me, and I do not blame him. Men of his nature deal in a world where everything is shady, and no one is truth worthy. When he extends his hand to seal the agreement, I do not shake it. He does not take offense; he probably does not want to touch me either.

With only a few hours before departure, I decide to purify my body in preparation for entering the river ocean. I traverse the old town until finding a traditional hammam tucked away in a side alley. The gloomy-eyed attendant does not ask any questions nor does he demand any money. He simply points in the direction of the room where I am supposed to disrobe. The air inside the space feels heavy; a mixture of vapor and smoke forms a tangible curtain in front of my eyes. I then recognize the sweet smell of burnt opium, thick and rich, like a flower on fire. I remember frequenting places like this in Marrakech before taking shelter behind the red door. I remember them well. After carefully removing my tunic, I follow the narrow hallway to a small room clad in white stone where the vapor is even denser. Here I will rest my body; here I will release all the impurities that dealing with people has forced inside of me.

Time then becomes immemorial. I feel as if everything that has ever happened to me occurred centuries ago. I look into the abyss of my past, and the immense void gives me a sense of vertigo. I close my eyes, and I breathe. I inhale the warm vapor. When I look into the abyss again, it seems to grow, to unfold further. I lie down on my back, and the heat radiating from the moist white stone penetrates my body. The heat flows through me. And I feel as if every molecule composing my body vibrates slightly, creating space around them, letting go of anything clinging to them. I feel the rivers of unwanted thoughts, toxins, memories, and fears flow away from my body. I am being vacated.

I think of what awaits me. An immersion into the river ocean. A likely immersion into my past. A probable confirmation that my past is moribund. A telling of tales, a telling of stories. An unraveling of the writer's true fears. A vigilance for the obscure vices of the bearded captain. A vision of Essaouira. A landing on the ocean sand. A long walk towards the desert sand. An encounter with the unknown. Or perhaps, what truly awaits me is nothing at all. Maybe an intimate vision of the bright moon and a simple exchange of breaths with the river ocean. My body cannot tell me, and my mind, in playful intercourse with the vapors in this room, slackens its grip on reality.

Once I become aware of my breath again, once I start to feel my body, I realize the immediacy of my journey. I make my way through the misty spaces and find my tunic, my only shelter, awaiting me. My purified body accepts the shelter, and as a unity of interiority and exteriority, I leave the hammam and head for the stone bench in front of the ocean. I fear the day has escaped me; that time has moved faster than I expected. But when I reach the stone bench, the sun has not reached its apex yet, and the writer is nowhere. I then re-establish the order of time and wait a few minutes before high noon.

The writer strikes twelve steps as he approaches the bench. He comes to face various levels of uncertainty. A brave man he is. On his face, I notice a certain degree of apprehension, but at the same time, a glimmer of inquisitiveness. Does he exercise his free will when coming on this journey? I am not sure. I believe he needs to come. A force outside his consciousness must be at work in his mind. Otherwise, if he were entirely sensible, he would have changed course and rejected this journey. But there is a path we all follow, our very own path, informed by everything within ourselves, and by the universe around us.

—What brings you back here?

—You asked me to be here at noon.

—Yes, but that doesn't mean you had to come.

—It's my choice.

—Is it really your choice, or does it feel like it is your choice?

—At this very moment, I wouldn't know the difference.

—Then, you're looking for more words.

—Words mean the world when the world means little to me. That's all I can say.

And that is all he says. The writer follows me to the port without asking any questions. He walks with the same determination as when he walked all the way from Lisbon to Cádiz. He wanted something then; he needed to find his inner beast. And today is no different. He clearly needs something, even if he is not completely aware of the nature of the need. When we arrive at the port, we find the bearded captain sitting in the cockpit of his sailboat smoking a cigar. He takes a good look at the writer, at myself, and I imagine he doubts whether we are capable of managing our duties as crew. Or maybe he is setting a price on our heads. He tosses what is left of the cigar in the water and invites us to come on board.

The captain does not ask for our names nor does he ask for passports or any identification. He goes around the boat as if we do not exist, making sure everything is ready for departure. He checks all the lines, the winches, the sails. I move towards the bow, from where a gentle breeze is coming, and my tunic starts to flap like a loose sail. At once the captain demands that I move downwind to the stern. He says it is safer there, but I think he has other reasons. When he finishes making all sort of preparations, the captain comes back to the cockpit and sits across from me. He lights another cigar and begins to smoke, placidly disconnecting himself from everything around him. This may be how he deals with his own insecurities before taking to the sea. He inhales and exhales his fears.

The wind begins to die down, and the captain emerges from the seance with his own demons. He takes advantage of the quiet wind to hoist the mainsail and release the boom. With the sail flapping slightly, he lets go of the spring lines, and the gentle breeze pushes the boat away from the dock. Then he trims the mainsail and unwinds the jib. As the boat starts to sail into the ocean, I watch the face of the writer. I cannot decipher what he may be feeling at this time, but I know that deep inside him a tempest of words is brewing.

Part IV
The Red Door

The striped tunic

Around me, there is no visible land, only the vast horizon extending in a circular way. No matter which way I look, at the very far end the ocean touches the sky. Without my feet touching the ground I feel displaced. I know where the land is: one hundred meters below the hull of this boat or two days ahead at the shores of Essaouira. And the fluidity of the space engulfing me allows my mind to drift securely, freely, with no encroaching limits. Floating in silence, I take the risk to delve into a few deep recesses of my memory. Nothing at first, just a dim light over a milky white surface. I try to break that white surface with my thoughts, but they fail to puncture it, they simply slide away. I must be patient.

The writer has not spoken since he boarded the boat. He has not written a single word either. He must be accumulating visions and sounds. I wonder if he also accumulates ideas, philosophical propositions, unanswered questions. I also wonder if he lives his life separately from the life of his books. Are they one and the same? A thorny proposition that would be. But somehow he must die a little with each book he writes. Or perhaps, he gives a little of himself with every book. That would also be dangerous since after writing several books there would be nothing left of himself. If that were the case, writing would be an exercise in self-annihilation. No, he would not go to that extent to obliterate himself. Perhaps he lives a more extensive, larger, and deeper life because of his books. If so, most engaged minds would choose to write books. Ergo, they would come to face their inner beast. There is the fear. And the fear makes him break his silence for he begins to speak.

—Where are we going?

—Does it matter?

—I'm sure it matters to someone; you, or the captain…

—Does it matter to you?

—It does, but it doesn't.

—Then you must be in the middle of writing about something crucial.

—I'm writing what I need to write.

—And what determines what you need to write?

—Life, what happens around me, everything…

—What's around you right now is the river ocean, the captain, and myself.

—That's precisely the reason why I'm here.

—So, then, our destination is of no consequence to you.

The captain keeps his distance. He is essentially sailing the boat by himself and does not seem eager to ask for help. And this worries me for I expected he would like to exploit us. For the moment he seems content to manage the boat on his terms, he gives no orders and no explanations. I assume he follows the agreed course south to Essaouira, an assumption I better confirm before nightfall.

The wind starts to accelerate, and the waves begin to grow. The boat responds with brisk movements that make it necessary for us to hold on tight. The captain gets a wide grin on his face and chews on a few words I cannot understand. He then asks me to hold on to a line and to pull as hard as I can when told. He prepares to tack. When he steers the bow across the wind, he screams at me to pull the line. I pull hard and the boat heels to an uncomfortable angle. The captain's grin widens. He takes the line from me and fastens it to the winch. He then hands the wheel to the writer and tells him to keep a steady course. And without saying anything else, he disappears belowdecks.

The boat inserts its bow into the conversation between the wind and the ocean. It glides forward interrupting the eternal discourse. The ocean responds by sending spray up in the air for the wind to catch and throw at us. It is not an angry response; it is an invitation to join in the conversation. I would speak to the river ocean just like I have spoken to the air in Marrakech—with honesty. They know my secrets although I cannot decipher theirs. But unlike men, they will never divulge what has been whispered in their ear. We will speak to each other in the quiet of the night. I have two long nights before landfall to converse, to speak my memory.

—Do you know the direction in which you're steering?

—The sun is ahead of us; we must be heading south.

—True at this time of the day. But what if it were a red sun instead?

—I imagine west.

—And in the dark, which way would you steer?

—I would pick a star and follow it.

—How about the path ahead of you? Can you see it?

—All I see in front of me is water, and the horizon bending far away.

—That's because there's no inherent path. You make the path as you go.

—But if I turn around, I can see the boat leaving a wake behind us.

—That path vanishes, and you'll never step on that same path again.

—So, there's no path.

—There has never been one.

A natural rhythm settles the boat and our minds. Nothing seems to change, while at the same time, everything is changing. The ocean carries our weight on its supple back, the wind opens its arms, and the sun looks down with casual interest. And we carry on leaving no trace or memory of our passage. A few minutes ago we existed, as we exist this very moment. What happened in between that moment and now could be a memory. But if we are not interested in recalling it, then nothing happened between then and now. Just the boat gliding through the vastness. Perhaps the passage of time is different on solid ground. Perhaps the magnitude of our impact is larger as we traverse forests, meadows, or sand. But our legacy cannot only be a solid imprint, like a fossil. Our legacy has to include the immaterial imprint on our mind and the minds of others. Time, then, is marked by what we feel and by what others make us feel.

The captain emerges from belowdecks with an air of boredom. He makes his way forward and sits with his legs dangling over the toe rail. With some difficulty, he lights a cigar and the white smoke blends with the wind. For a long while, he remains there, taking puffs from his cigar without looking aft, refusing to engage with the writer or me. And from time to time he looks far ahead as if trying to find a landfall, or perhaps another vessel. Then, suddenly, he starts singing in a language I do not recognize. But I do not need to understand the words to tell he is hurting. It is a deep and dark melody, heartfelt as if mourning an object of desire. He carries the tune to the end after which he goes back to his former silence. I wonder how he relates to the ocean, to his past, to his pain… The wind extinguishes the cigar. He tries to light what remains of the cigar but fails to do so. He takes a good look at the truncated cigar as if studying its physiognomy, and after whispering a few words, he tosses it into the water. He continues to look out to the horizon, but I wonder if his eyes are open.

After a while, the captain comes aft to the cockpit and looks at the compass. He inspects the shape of the sails carefully, the tell-tales. After trimming the main and the jib only so slightly, he takes hold of the wheel. He makes a minor correction to the course the boat is heading and hands me the wheel this time. In a low and morose voice, he tells me to keep the course steady until dawn. I regard his face for a second, and what I encounter is an empty expression. He simply looks abandoned. Then he turns around and buries himself belowdecks under the weight of his emptiness. I have seen men like him in the desert, unattached, floating over a thin and fragile life.

—My dear writer, the course is already set.

—I'm not a writer today.

—What are you then if not a writer?

—I'm the path.

—I thought we had agreed there's no path.

—I'm the path but not in the sense of a trail, a walkway, or an alley. I'm a channel.

—And what goes through you?

—Your past goes through me.

—My past is barely breathing.

—Speak your past then, before it suffocates.

—Where are you going with this?

—You probably know. You said the course is already set.

Calixto

They started to land on his awareness, the words, in rhythmic coincidence, with the same soft undulations as the waves that struck the boat amidships. The striped tunic had dislodged a narrative starting with events that occurred in forsaken corners of the Algerian Desert. He spoke in a calm voice, precise, without undue affectations. People in his story were referred to by name or attributes. Sometimes the only description a person would receive was a state of mind, as if someone could only exist as the embodiment of anger, jealousy, or bliss. Other times people were described by their actions: the murderer, the bearer of fortune, the wind gatherer. Places were named using the local dialect, often ancient names, or by their geographical relation to another place, or by their climate. But the essential characteristic of the narrative was that events seemed interconnected in ways that were obvious, sometimes, but in deeply obtuse ways other times. He was recounting an entire cosmogony of people, places, and events.

Calixto did nothing but listen to the narrative and try to feel as the striped tunic felt during the recounted events. He was not afraid of missing details or particular twists in the story. He knew very well that his own memory would reconstruct the narrative and employ ample license in the process. But what mattered to him most was the emotional charge attached to the events. That was the past worth recovering, the feelings elicited inside the striped tunic and in those around him when everything took place. The rest could be replaced or even discarded, but those feelings were precious.

In a metaphorical and poetic way, the striped tunic was offering not so much answers to particular questions about his past, but ways of beginning to think about his past. He was peeling off his tunic and revealing his naked self, tender and vulnerable. He spoke uninterruptedly for several hours, and he did so candidly as if nobody but the ocean could listen to his confessions. And when the moon rose, the striped tunic had only reached the early stages of his journey.

The night ushered a truce between the wind and the ocean. They both recoiled and left a clear and calm realm for the boat to traverse. And the voice of the striped tunic acquired a diaphanous transparency making his narrative take flight under the moonlight. What seemed overwhelming in the early evening hours, the complexity of the narrative lines had become more and more understandable as the night deepened. Calixto was developing a mental map of a past that did not belong to him, but in the exercise of its recreation, that past was assuming life anew, it began to breathe, to exist once more. And he knew those words would be dispersed by the breeze, that the chance they would be heard again in the order and cadence imparted by the striped tunic was practically null. In the absolute night, Calixto understood he was the only witness to the miracle.

Soon after the morning broke, the captain made his appearance on deck. He did not bother to greet anyone. He moved around verifying the boat was in proper order and on the right course. Then he went belowdecks for a while after which he emerged with coffee and bread. He served himself first and then invited Calixto and the striped tunic to partake. He said a few inaudible words without expecting a response. It seemed evident he knew their exact location and where they were heading. This was a familiar passage for him, and his apparent boredom revealed so. He confirmed once again the course and told them both not to change anything, to keep a firm hand on the wheel, and to alert him if any other vessel showed up in the horizon. Then he vanished down the hatch.

Calixto took charge of the wheel. The striped tunic went forward and lay down in front of the mast. There he rested his body but not his mind. He started to sing what seemed like an epic poem. For a moment Calixto thought he heard the words of Homer, that the events narrated were those of the Odyssey. But as he paid attention, he realized the story was a continuation of what the striped tunic had recounted the night before. Recited in dactylic hexameter, the simplicity, speed, and directness of the narrative, the brilliance, and excitement of the action, and the imposing humanity of the characters disarmed him. He wanted to listen to the striped tunic for the next one hundred years; he wanted to travel on that boat as far as the farthest corner of the ocean.

And then the wind began to blow harder. The small waves became longer, and the white horses started to gallop on the surface of the ocean. Then the waves began to rise and crest over. And foam blew in streaks along the direction of the wind. The boat heeled aggressively, and Calixto had to firm up his grip on the wheel. In the midst of the wind force, the striped tunic stood up and held on to the mast. He pushed his back against the mast and braced himself by holding on as hard as he could. And with his chest open towards the bow, he continued to recite the epical poem of his past. The turbulent wind and the excited words intoxicated Calixto. And for a moment, he thought he had witnessed immortality.

As the hours matured, the wind gradually calmed its temper. The boat sailed south by southwest at a steady and comfortable rhythm. The voice of the striped tunic had not ceased for a minute during the course of the day. He had sustained the arch of a fascinating story that revealed a dense past, worthy of a thousand lives. But what fascinated Calixto the most was the inner workings of the striped tunic's mind. He had never imagined that a mind could have such a deep understanding of other people's minds. His epic poem revealed a significant gift for intuition, but an even more powerful capacity for observation. He was capable of distilling a person's ultimate fears. And once Calixto realized that he had been followed, observed, and spoken to by that piercing mind, he felt completely naked and exposed. He felt transparent.

Up in the sky, the clouds became thinner and thinner until they were no longer. There was a clarity of light that made the late afternoon resemble the morning. But soon enough the color red started infiltrating the horizon far to the west. Calixto kept looking ahead, thinking he would see land arise over the horizon. But nothing materialized. Another night of sailing would follow, and in that night the striped tunic's story would grow and deepen. Calixto was afraid his memory would not be capable of containing the epic tale. He was afraid of forgetting what the striped tunic was afraid to forget himself. Without control of that journey, without faith on his capacity to recall, without a clear sense of what would happen upon landing, transparent as he felt that moment, Calixto let go of the wheel, and the boat turned immediately to the wind. The sails began to luff at once, and the boat got trapped in irons.

Soon enough the captain made his appearance on deck. His bored air had not changed. His eyes seemed heavy as if tired of watching an ocean that did not mean anything to him. He did not seem interested in what had happened; he only asked if they had seen another vessel. When nobody responded to his question, he took the time to look out in all directions to confirm they were alone in the visible confines. He then set the boat once again on its course and gave the wheel to the striped tunic. He said the night would be calm, that if they kept the course, they would reach Essaouira in the morning hours, and if they kept their mouths shot nothing bad would happen. He then took a long look at the striped tunic, and he could not help contain his disgust. He coughed, he grabbed his throat as if choking, and he went belowdecks almost head first.

That was the beginning of the longest night Calixto would ever experience. He was about to face a density of time commensurate with the density of the emotional story the striped tunic would unleash that night. And it all started with a revelation of vulnerability when the striped tunic spoke about his fear of dying. When Calixto asked what he meant by death, the striped tunic explained that death had nothing to do with the loss of life, but with the loss of an emotional past. He went on to clarify that there was a feeble past, the one that contained vacuous events, maybe multiple vacuous events, but all devoid of an emotional connection. That past could be recounted, even chronicled, but meant nothing and could not really die because it had no life, to begin with. Then there was the past made of a deep emotional fiber. That past had touched someone at an unconscious level; it had penetrated the deepest rooms of the mind and caused inner vibrations. That past was alive, even if the person had no memory of it. And that was the past worth unearthing, recalling, immortalizing.

The striped tunic held on to the wheel and kept a steady course. The ocean kept coming at them, and so did the night, and the wind. And as if speaking to the universe at large, the striped tunic continued to recount the most improbable story Calixto had ever imagined. And as the night extended its reach beyond that of the hours, time lost its essence. The words coming from the striped tunic's mouth interlaced with the voluminous words emerging from the very ocean. And what was told was told as a unity of nature. Mind, emotion, time, life, and death were all existing on the same plane. And the story was not the story of a man or a woman, of a country or a continent, but the story of the emotions of all who live and have lived on the face of the earth.

The boat glided over the silky waters leaving no trace of its passage. The moon rose and fell into the ocean without making any sound. The wind continued to circle around the earth. The birds began to approach the boat wondering why. And the minds of Calixto and the striped tunic were one with the words. At that time, far ahead in the horizon, toward where the sun had started to usher the day, there was the vision of land emerging.

The striped tunic

The golden walls of Essaouira try to split a land from its ocean. A fruitless effort for no structure rooted in land can keep the air from flowing free. Like in my courtyard of Marrakech where the air visited at will. And with the air come the sounds and the smells. Sometimes the howling of the beast can be heard throughout the village when carried by the innocent air from one open courtyard to the next. For those who observe and listen, the lives of others are always present under the open sky.

As the boat approaches the port, there is yet no sign of the captain, and I wonder what his intentions are. I cannot steer and dock the boat. Neither can the writer. The ocean begins to boil at the mouth of the port making the course of the boat erratic. I try to control the situation by turning the wheel right and left, but the wild movement of the boom makes it impossible. We are bobbing up and down with no clear direction. And soon we start to come close to other boats that sail in and out of the port.

The thrashing must have alerted the captain who now comes to take hold of the wheel. He maneuvers well enough to rectify the course, and we find ourselves heading straight for the dock. The captain yells a few orders. He hands me a line and tells me to stand by the bow. He hands the writer another line and asks him to stand by the stern. He then glides slowly inside the port and comes alongside the dock. At once he jumps on the dock and asks us to throw the lines to him. He fastens both lines, and the boat comes to rest. But as soon as the captain has secured the lines, two men in uniform come to greet him.

The three men argue, they gesticulate. I feel the hostility between them. The men in uniform stand next to each other and block the only access to land on the dock. The captain finds himself trapped between the two men in front of him and the water behind him. Then, in a flanking maneuver, the men in uniform get on each side of the captain and escort him off the dock. They disappear through an opening in the golden wall. And I get a sense this is only the beginning, or perhaps the end, depending on the perspective. I ask the writer to go belowdecks and to remain silent. Then I sit in the cockpit and wait. There are times when a man lets adversity come to find him, and those are always better than the times when he goes out to find adversity himself.

After some time, the two men in uniform return to the boat. They come without the captain, which leads me to believe he has encountered some adversity of his own. They board the boat without asking permission and come to stand in front of me. The expression on their faces is not serene; they seem anxious, or bothered by doing what they probably do not want to do. They expect me to start talking, but I remain as quiet as I am wise.

—Where do you come from?

—I come from everywhere, and toward everywhere I go. But as the uninvited, perhaps you could tell me where the two of you come from?

—We're the ones who ask questions here.

—Does that preclude you from answering?

—What does "preclude" mean?

—It means to prohibit or to arrest you from doing something.

—We do that, we prohibit, and we arrest.

—So, you're not arrested, are you?

—No, no, no… we're the ones who arrest other people.

—Therefore, you can go ahead and answer.

—Let's be clear. We're the ones who ask, and you're the one who answers.

—That's perfect. What would you like to know?

—Where did you meet the captain?

—I don't know the captain.

—But you're in his boat.

—I don't know if this boat belongs to him.

—Ok. What brought you here?

—The boat did.

At this point, the breeze turns around and starts to blow inland. The two uniformed men look at each other and step away from me. They take a minute before continuing with their questions.

—What's your land?

—The desert.

—There're many deserts.

—Not really. There's only one desert where all the sands coalesce.

—Coalesce?

—Yes, join together, combine, mingle.

—Forget the mingling for now; we're not getting any closer to you. Where do you intend to go from here?

—I want to go to where my past feels safe.

—What does that mean?

—It means nothing to you, but the world to me.

The two men turn their backs and confer with each other. The breeze takes their voices away. Then they disembark without saying anything else to me. They walk down the dock and disappear again through the opening in the golden wall. I wait for a few minutes, and neither the captain nor the two men in uniform come back to the boat. I then ask the writer to gather himself and to prepare for a long walk. And, as hastily as possible, we leave the boat behind, the port, the ocean. We traverse the ancient village avoiding any contact, like the fugitives we are not. I walk ahead this time, and the writer follows me. And as we head east, I recognize the fresh scent of flowering orange trees.

Marrakech, Marrakech, why do you haunt me? I found refuge within your walls; I contained my impulses behind the red door. And then death happened, as it does, without asking. Would the fountain still sing to me? Would the air feel free to visit? Would there be another tender soul wanting to touch me? That was then, and there is no certainty that it would be the same now. To the contrary, everything already experienced is by definition consumed, extinct. And that is the problem with the past, that we keep on murdering it as we move along. But perhaps what remains alive is what we felt. I know how it felt when the fountain sang to me, that has not died, it reverberates inside of me. I can still feel the sensation of touching somebody. I can still feel the moist seduction of mint tea traveling through my throat and releasing a certain goodness. I also felt fear when persecuted. And when I instilled fear on others, I was then afraid of my own self. I felt all of that.

Reaching Marrakech is a question for which I have no answer. It is a desire based on the fallibility of the present day. It is the need to look into the precipice. And if I keep on walking east, climbing the gentle hills, I will reach the plateau from where the desert extends with the majesty of an ocean. Then, through the clear desert air, my eyes will confront the spectacle of the Atlas Mountains. At their foothills, I will find Marrakech in its redness. But that encounter will happen in the future, a time devoid of emotional experience, a time that has yet to be lived. I cannot predict the wounds that will be inflicted on any mind once I reach Marrakech. And even more obscure, how would I feel about those wounds?

And as the day becomes the night, and the night becomes the day, we sustain our march. A silent march this is, for the writer and I have not exchanged a word since we both set foot on dry land. I am aware of his need for words, the sole desire that seems to propel him forward. In which case he must be suffering at this very moment. But perhaps he aims for more than words and a story to tell. Perhaps he just wants to touch immortality like most living things. Or perhaps, he needs to write in order to exist in this world that grants no reason for existence. I cannot decipher the pure essence of his need. And for that very reason, I am content to walk and hear him walk behind me, for I know he is wrestling with the beast inside of him.

Calixto

Once he saw the red stones guarding the entrance to the ancient city, Calixto understood that people had disputed their right to belong inside those walls for generations. And he also understood he had no right to the terrain inside the mind of the striped tunic. He had listened and memorized the epic tale, but he had no right to narrate that story as his own. An apocryphal writer he would be if he were to simply write what he had heard over the past few days. Furthermore, his story would not resemble the true life of the striped tunic. He had no chance of reaching the inner confines of his mind. The narrative would then have no merit; it would not honor the very reason of its existence. He then realized he was in possession of an extraordinary wealth of words he could not handle. So when in front of Bab Agnaou, the gate to the eternal city, he stopped walking altogether and stood facing the afternoon sun.

The striped tunic stood next to him, calmly, and did not ask the reason for halting his march. They both admired the gate and the surrounding redness. And when the striped tunic asked him if he was ready to drop all expectations and enter the city as a child, a child that had yet to write his first few lines, Calixto answered that he was indeed nubile, for at no other time in his life had he felt so naked. And together they crossed the Bab Agnaou and pierced the core of the ancient city. And the walls grew around them, and the narrow streets channeled their steps, and the sounds of people living their lives, transacting with each other, loving one another, vibrated in the dry desert air. Inside the walls of Marrakech, Calixto felt vulnerable.

They walked in what Calixto thought were concentric circles. The alleys turned always to the left even when a right turn would have offered a more inviting option. But for Calixto, the difference between one option or another had virtually disappeared. He was at the mercy of the striped tunic, who was at the mercy of his own tumultuous memories, or at best, at the mercy of his sequestered passions. And as the day lengthened its reach, the march through the village had become an enigma. And when Calixto was about to halt his march again, they reached the fabled Djemaa El-Fna with the snake charmers, acrobat monkeys, storytellers, musicians, and dancers. Here Calixto was assaulted by the confluence of a thousand stories. All of them vibrant, engaging. Words were rising and clamoring, a frenetic exchange of meanings was traversing the square from corner to corner. And Calixto understood the greatness of this source, a source of words that could challenge that of the ocean.

Exhausted, both men lay on the ground next to a pile of oranges that would likely be sold in the morning hours. They had no words for each other; they simply let the night traverse through them. But the night brought to Calixto's ears what he had never heard, or allow himself to hear: the wrenching, piercing howling of the beast, the horrid unconscious voice that haunts everyone, every night, in the deepest level of their somnolence. Frightened at first, Calixto bit his lip and braced himself. But as he listened to the lamenting voice of numerous beasts unknown to him, as the howling grew and multiplied, as he came in touch with a multitude of selves vying for expression in the empty hours of the night, he felt a certain lightness and calm.

He realized that he was not alone, that he bore no respon-
sibility for their suffering, but that he could be, perhaps,
their verbal conduit. And as Calixto and the striped tunic
remained prostrated in their sleep, the night continued to
deepen and the beasts continued to howl.

The striped tunic

Dawn makes a raucous arrival when it unleashes several layers of wind on the Djemaa El-Fna. The merchants have to secure their wares, and more than one yells a blasphemous word. The violence of the untouchable substance touches every single person occupying the square. And the prayer from the nearby minaret is severely dismantled. I speak to the writer and tell him we need to find a red door, but he only hears the brutal sound of the wind. So fluid, so invisible, so malleable, yet so destructive. I grab onto my tunic and start to walk toward the narrow streets of the Medina without saying anything else to the writer. And when he realizes that motion is imminent, he gets on his feet and follows after me.

I know where the red door is and what lies behind it. I know there will be four flowering orange trees standing in the corners of the courtyard. Would they remember me in the same way I remember them, with affection? Or would I be nothing to them like I am nothing to the rest of the world? I think the fountain will still be singing, but what would the song be? And what I cannot unravel are the desires behind the red door. Or perhaps, more realistically, the desires inside my own mind. Arriving in Marrakech a second time is not a return; it is a continuation of the same search I started within the heart of the desert. Do we ever change as people? Maybe our fears are the ones that change.

I walk aimlessly through the old streets and find enormous satisfaction in not being recognized. My striped tunic is only one among many, and my face so ragged, so anonymous. I move as fluidly as the wind among people. I could flow as a simple conscience. And as such, I expand over the roofs of the Medina, and I breathe once again the air that sustained me for so long, before the deaths, before the impetus to flee. The writer must sense my inherent need for he asks no questions; he follows me unambiguously at a close distance. I imagine he intuits my need to make peace with my dying past, a past I spoke to him in full detail. If he was repulsed by it, he would have killed me already.

The shadows advance with the hours. And with each step, I come closer to the inevitable encounter with the threshold of my past. And that threshold, where my past and present come together, is no different from the threshold where the ocean meets the sky. They are both inaccessible; we can pursue them knowing we will never touch them. But they exist nonetheless, and we bow to them. So I begin to correct my path and veer in the direction of the red door. I traverse familiar squares and nefarious streets, I enter the womb of the Medina, I hear the clamor of words I now ignore, and I pierce the final alley at which end stands a red door.

—Is this a dead end?

—No, this is the beginning of my future.

—But this alley leads nowhere.

—It is what's behind this red door that concerns me.

—What's behind it?

—Everything that I've started to forget and everything that you can't help but write down.

I look at the writer, and I get the impression I am looking at myself. I think of my past, the time that has elapsed up until this instant, and I think of the time that is yet to come. And with utmost care and deliberate gestures, I remove my striped tunic and torn sandals. I extend my arms and offer them to the writer. Without saying a word, the writer gets rid of his clothes and dons the striped tunic and the sandals. And I speak to him for the last time.

—Where would you go next?

—I need the backing of the ocean.

—To write or to dream?

—To exist.

—Then go away from yourself, but close to shore and even closer to your feelings.

—I'm going back to Lisbon.

—And what can Lisbon offer you?

—Bread and a salamander.

After listening to his words, I turn my back on the writer and face the red door. I push the red door open and step through it in full nakedness. Inside there is a courtyard with a fountain in the center. In each of the four corners of the courtyard, there is a flowering orange tree vibrating with life.

JORGE ARMENTEROS was born in Cuba, his family leaving for Madrid, Spain, then Tampa, Florida, before finally settling in Puerto Rico. After graduating cum laude from Harvard University, he acquired an MD at the University of Puerto Rico, an MA in Spanish and Latin American Literature at New York University, and an MFA in Creative Writing at Lesley University. Armenteros is the author of the 2015 International Latino Book Award winner *The Book of I* (Jaded Ibis Press), and the first two books of the *Striped Tunic Trilogy*: *Air* and *The Roar of the River* (Spuyten Duyvil Press). Armenteros resides in the South of France.

www.ingramcontent.com/pod-product-compliance
Lightning Source LLC
Chambersburg PA
CBHW050510190726
48284CB00003B/760